Some of my Favorite

Sherlockian Things

A Compendium of Pawky and Outré

Monographs, Toasts and Whatnots

By

E.A. (Bud) Livingston

First edition published in 2016

Paperback ISBN 978-1-78092-962-0
ePub ISBN 978-1-78092-963-7
PDF ISBN 978-1-78092-964-4

Published in the UK by MX Publishing
335 Princess Park Manor, Royal Drive,
London, N11 3GX
www.mxpublishing.co.uk

Cover design by Brian Belanger

Acknowledgments

A big thank you to Warren Randall, Bob Katz,
George Vandenburgh

And

Doris Lehman, my extraordinary partner who
continues to be extraordinary

NOTE: Canon titles are referenced by standard abbreviations, which are listed on the back page. For example, "CROO" is the abbreviation for "The Crooked Man." THE "(A)" prior to the title stands for "The adventures of."

Table of Contents

Introduction

Oscar Hammerstein wrote:

Rain drops on roses and whiskers on kittens

Bright copper kettles and warm woolen mittens

Brown paper packages tied up with strings

These are a few of my favorite things

I wrote:

A tall thin detective

With strength in his fingers

He ponders, deduces, but also malingers

Small cardboard boxes

Tied up with strings

These are my favorite Sherlockian things

The sculptor Meuniere,

Ronald Adair,

And Mary, John's most patient wife,

Dunbar on the docket

And in Straker's pocket

We'll soon find a cataract knife

Operatic contraltos and Bohemian Kings
These are my favorite Sherlockian things

When the dog bites
And the bee stings
When I'm feeling sad
I simply remember Sherlockian things
And then I don't feel so bad

Bright Copper Beeches and
Bitterns a-booming
A fierce, fiery Hound
Disaster is looming
Jacobson's Yard, Inspector Lestrade
The mean Baron Gruner's romantical flings
These are my favorite Sherlockian things

The feared Evans Pott
And Grimesby Roylott
Villains without parallel

The small rajah's gems

A chase on the Thames

An Andaman Islander from Hell

A bedroom pull without rings

These are my favorite Sherlockian things

When my stocks stall

When the Mets fall

When I'm feeling sad

I simply remember Sherlockian things and

Then I don't feel so bad.

The man on the Tor

The Sign of the Four

A fierce Cecil Barker

Jew's-harp-playing Parker

The Reigate Squires

The camp of McQuires

Hatty Doran

The creep-creeping man

The good news that Holmes often brings

These are my favorite Sherlockian things

When the friends go

And I feel low

And I pull the blanket over my head

I simply remember Sherlockian things and

Then I feel good instead

Chapter 1

How I became a Sherlockian

I was introduced to Sherlock Holmes in 1939 when a bunch of us, all around 9 or 10, trouped to the Marine Theater on Flatbush Avenue, in Brooklyn, to see The Hound of the Baskervilles, with Basil Rathbone and Nigel Bruce, but starring Richard Green. This was the best of this series as it followed rather closely the original story line. It seemed evident that none of our parents knew just how scary this movie was and how much trauma it produced in our young minds. Fast forward to 1952 when I was stationed on the jungle side of the Panama Canal, at Fort Sherman, with little to do. Someone loaned me the Complete Works of Sherlock Holmes and I made another mistake. I began reading The Valley of Fear, a scary tale of the Molly McGuires of the coal mines and of the brave Pinkerton agent who lived with the cutthroats and murderers in Eastern Pennsylvania. This, one of the four Sherlockian novels, has the greatest denouement of all, and it frightened the life out of me. I could not sleep that night anticipating the ending and I wound up in the latrine at 2 a.m., vowing not to read any more Sherlock Holmes at night.

Is Birdy Edwards here? Yes, I am Birdy Edwards!!!

I belong to several Sherlockian clubs, called scions, where we discuss, argue and have fun with the Canon, as we call the works of Sherlock Holmes. The Scions are generally named after something in the Canon. When Holmes first came up to London he took rooms on Montague Street. So the group in Brooklyn meets on Montague Street. One case involves the Priory School and so there is a scion in Manhattan called The Priory School Scholars, the first group I joined. Watson observes that Holmes has a "practical but limited knowledge of geology," so there is a group in Denver called The Practical But Limited Geologists. One case is called The Three Garridebs and so the scion in Westchester County is The Three Garridebs and the presiding officers have adopted the individual names of those Garridebs.

Sherlockians are funny people. The case of the Three Garridebs involves a search for anyone named Garrideb, almost a unique name, to fulfill the demands of a peculiar will in Kansas worth 5 million dollars. One enterprising member, a telephone company employee, actually put a listing for Arthur Garrideb in the Westchester phone book until someone let this secret out of the bag and he had to delete it in the next edition of the directory. A woman started a scion in San Francisco named after the case of the Solitary Cyclist. She was the only member.

When I visited Australia in 1996 I met Phil Cornell, the official artist of the Sydney Passengers group. He invited me to his home and on one of his walls I saw movie posters for the <u>Hound of the Baskervilles</u> starring Basil Rathbone and Nigel Bruce.

As I walked on I saw posters for <u>A Study in Scarlet</u>, <u>The Sign of Four</u>, and <u>The Valley of Fear</u>, all featuring these two stars. Phil,

I said, I don't recall who made those last three movies. No one did, he answered. I just made up the posters!

Each scion is different. Some have luncheons some do not. Some have toasts and games which can be very funny. The Epilogues, in Chatham, New Jersey, selects two cases and dissects them and it is interesting to hear the different takes on each case,

Often I hear a side I hadn't thought of before.

And that is just one description of a Sherlockian.

Chapter 2

Monographs

Elias Openshaw's Civil War Connection With the Ku Klux Klan

"My uncle," said John Openshaw, "emigrated to America when he was a young man and became a planter in Florida, where he was reported to have done very well. At the time of the war he fought in Jackson's army, and afterwards under Hood, where he rose to be a colonel." (FIVE)

Who was Jackson? Who was Hood? And what about the curious incident concerning Nathan Bedford Forrest? Forrest is never mentioned, yet he did plenty, even in the nighttime. And it is he who is involved in the demise of Elias Openshaw.

Jackson was Thomas Jonathan Jackson, known as Stonewall, and even today, 153 years after his fatal wounding during the battle of Chancellorsville in May 1863, he remains one of the most famous soldiers in American history; his campaigns in the Shenandoah Valley are still studied today in military schools worldwide. With his small army, known as foot cavalry because of their long, forced marches, Jackson wreaked havoc among a series of Union generals who commanded larger forces. His presence, even his alleged presence, frightened the Lincoln administration to the point that it withheld troops from other generals in order to protect Washington from him. Jackson's flank march during the battle of Chancellorsville rolled up the

Federal XI Corps and set the stage for the most brilliant Confederate victory of the war. It was after this amazing success that, in the twilight, he and his aides were taken for Union soldiers and fired upon. "Old Blue Light," as his men called him, was mortally wounded.

Jackson had had an amazing symbiotic relationship with his commanding officer, Robert E. Lee, always anticipating what Lee wanted done. His loss proved to be painful for the Confederate cause as his absence during the battle of Gettysburg may have been a major factor for the lack of Confederate success there. Jackson was secretive and devious, always trying to confuse and bewilder his more numerous enemies, and usually succeeding.

In contrast, John Bell Hood was a slugger. This giant Kentuckian led his troops from the front; there was nothing subtle about him. Interestingly enough, Hood lost his right leg during the battle of Chickamauga and this injury put him into a group of other Canonical characters who had wooden legs: Jonathan Small (SIGN), Francis Prosper (BERY) and Josiah Amberley (RETI). When Confederate Joe Johnston's constant Fabian tactics (read retreat) failed to stop William T. Sherman's Western armies, Hood lobbied for Johnston's job as commander of the Army of Tennessee, a position he gained in July 1864. In this new command he inherited one of the most amazing soldiers of the Civil War, Nathan Bedford Forrest, who had an independent command of cavalry in that area. Practically bereft of schooling, Forrest had incredible natural abilities which made him the best known Rebel cavalry leader in the West and gained him the nom de guerre The Wizard of the Saddle. He, like Jackson, gained fame by whipping Union forces that continually outnumbered his troops, and his presence, just like Jackson's, awed his enemies. Forrest, amazingly, personally inflicted thirty casualties among Union soldiers, an unparalleled achievement for a combat leader. If Elias Openshaw had fought with Hood he would have known Forrest.

When the Postal System issued a series of Civil War stamps some twenty years ago, Forrest's portrait was missing. And his portrait will always be missing. Despite his fame and incredible abilities, Forrest's face will never adorn an American postage stamp.

Why?

Because he was the first Grand Wizard of the Ku Klux Klan. And that is the connection with Elias Openshaw.

Birth Control In The Canon

There is no mention of birth control, per se, in the Canon, although we may infer its practice, e.g. the widower Sir Charles Baskerville obviously had no children since his estate had to chase all the way to Canada to find an heir. The only specifically described childless couple was Colonel and Nancy Barclay, who had no children. I count twenty-one couples who, even though married for a long time, had no issue, as the lawyers would put it. Actually, being married and having no children proved to be downright dangerous. Of the twenty-one childless marriages, six wives die normally during the cases or are already dead, and they are the lucky ones: the two Mrs. Watsons, Mrs. Grimesby Roylott, Etta McMurdo (or Edwards), Mrs. Sir Charles Baskerville, and Mrs. Godfrey Staunton. Three wives meet, or had already met, violent deaths: Mrs. Adelbert Gruner, Mrs. Josiah Amberley, and Mrs. Jim Browner, while one wife literally pines away (Mrs. Lucy Ferrier Drebber).

A whole bunch of the childless husbands meet their maker in a variety of violent and bizarre manners: Grimesby Roylott, Jack Douglas, Sir Charles Baskerville, Colonel James Barclay, Sir Eustace Brackenstall, Hilton Cubitt, and Circus Owner Ronder. It seems it would be safer to remain single in Sherlock Holmes' England.

The next category is only children. There are thirty-one only children. How do we know? Well, the Canon either says so or we can infer it: Hattie Doran is an only child; Violet Hunter has no parents or relatives; Violet Smith was left without a relative in the world. Some are described as being "the only son" (Arthur Holder); "his only daughter" (Edith Presbury), et cetera. These people don't fare as badly as the childless couples as only two of them meet violent ends: John Openshaw and Cadogan West; but of the other only children, one is kidnapped and one is the kidnapper (Lord Saltire and James Wilder); one thinks he is a leper (Godfrey Emsworth); one is poisoned and another is the poisoner (Baby Ferguson and Little Jackie); one hires a hound from Hell to murder his long-lost relatives (Jack Baskerville Vandeleur Stapleton); one is accused unjustly of grand larceny (Arthur Holder); one almost marries a murderer (Violet DeMerville); one almost marries her stepfather (Mary Sutherland); one marries a couple of guys and becomes a bigamist (Hattie Doran); one loses his thumb (Victor Hatherley); one attempts suicide (Elsie Patrick Cubitt); one is locked away in a garret (Alice Rucastle) and three are accused of murder (James McCarthy, John Hector McFarlane and John Hopley Neligan).

Pairs of children (brothers, sisters, brother and sister) don't do much better. Of the twenty-two in this group, twelve die during the cases or prior to them, some in abnormal fashion. Others do dastardly things. Ronald Adair gets it with an air gun; Joseph Harrison turns traitor, Mary Fraser Brackenstall is abused with a hat pin; Paul Kratides won't sign his name but signs his death warrant instead; both the Pinners and the Randalls get caught; the Notting Hill murderer gets all chewed up; Sir James Walter drops dead while his brother Valentine sells secrets to enemy agents. And for God's sake, don't be a twin. Julia Stoner and Bartholomew Sholto meet their maker in fantastic ways. The youngest of the siblings to go seems to be poor Bob, Lucy Ferrier's brother, with Elias and Joseph Openshaw the oldest.

The three-children families include the Moriartys, the Cushings, and the Baskervilles. One sibling in each bunch died unnaturally, as did the covey of Tregennisses; the balance having gone bonkers. Another four-child family, the somewhat impoverished St. Simons, suffered little, except for their second son, the noblest, smuggest, unhappiest bachelor of them all. The luckiest family seems to consist of Sidney Johnson and his brood of five since nothing bad happens to them, and I am told that a certain gracious lady, although not mentioned by name, had nine children.

But who wins the prize for not practicing birth control? Well, it is never stated, but we can use our imagination again. This nasty individual had seven wives years before Jefferson Hope created a whole platoon of orphans. The winner just has to be our polygamous friend from Salt Lake City, Enoch Drebber, with his buddy Joseph Stangerson, at least a four-wifer, in second place.

Margaret Sanger would turn over in her grave.

The Boy From Oz

In The *Sign of Four*, Sherlock Holmes said, "When you observe the lower part of that watch-case you notice that it is not only dinted in two places, but it is cut and marked all over from the habit of keeping other hard objects, such as coins or keys, in the same pocket. Surely it is no great feat to assume that a man who treats a fifty-guinea watch so cavalierly must be a careless man. It is very customary for pawnbrokers in England when they take a watch to scratch the number of the ticket with a pin point upon the inside of the case. It is more handy than a label. There are no less than four such numbers visible to my lens on the inside of this case. Inference - that your brother was often at low water. Second inference - that he had occasional bursts of prosperity or he could not have redeemed the pledge. Finally I ask you to look at the inner plate, which contains the keyhole. Look at the thousands of scratches all round the hole - marks where the key has slipped. What sober man's key could have scored those grooves? But you will never see a drunkard's watch without them. He winds it at night and he leaves these traces in his unsteady hand. Where is the mystery in this? "

When James Armitage and Evans survived the rebellion and explosion on the Gloria Scott and were rescued by the Hotspur, they were not the only men in their lifeboat. Five prisoners and three sailors accompanied them as they shoved off from the Gloria Scott in the fashion of Captain Bligh of the Bounty.

Trevor never mentions the names of the three prisoners or three sailors. Or did he? I think he did and Holmes held back this information. One of those prisoners was none other than Hubert Wilson, convicted of public drunkenness, breaking into pawn-shops, and spitting in the Underground. Holmes knew his true name and withheld it from Watson. Trevor had mentioned it but Holmes did not want to cause Watson any pain and so held back this damning information. What Holmes knew is that the third prisoner had changed his name as did Armitage and Trevor. And Wilson, Holmes also knew, from Trevor's document, had changed his name to Watson and was none other than the father of John Hamish and Herman Watson. Armitage and Evans changed their names to Trevor and Beddoes, and prospered in the diggings of Australia while Wilson had the Levi Strauss concession in Victoria, selling dungarees with those great riveted pockets, to the miners. He made good money, married and raised two boys, but, reverting to his old ways, he maintained a friendship with John Barleycorn. He gambled away much of his fortune on the track, and all too often had to visit pawn shops in order to meet his mortgage each month. It seems that Hubert could not even wind his watch properly prior to bedtime. His hands trembled constantly and this behavior proved too much for his missus, a teetotaler. She left him when their children were small. Hubert was a good father, though, as he always took his boys with him during his deliveries of Levis to the miners at Ballarat where he chatted with his old cell-mates. He, too, like many Australians, did not like the educational facilities of his new country so he sent his sons to England for their schooling. Although they were always in

11

touch, Hubert never saw John and Herman again. At his death, he left the pittance he had saved, and his expensive watch, to John, and his collection of stamps and diggeradoo music to Herman. John, a middle sized, strongly built lad, with a square jaw and a thick neck, went to Blackheath junior college and met a variety of other Canonical characters in different schools, including Big Bob Ferguson and Percy Phelps. John capped his academic career by becoming a physician at the University of London, in a city where he had neither kith nor kin. His brother, Herman, went to Edinburgh to continue his education. He was mugged by a Scottish separatist in 1881 which left him in a weakened condition and he was unable to survive an avalanche in the Scottish Highlands. He willed the stamps and the diggeradoo collection to the Australian embassy. Holmes deduced that the timepiece belonged to Watson's unfortunate brother. That seemed obvious, but, in truth, it belonged to his unfortunate father. Watson was too embarrassed to tell this to Holmes since his detective friend had made a glaring error, something he did more often than Watson and Holmes liked to admit. Watson never mentioned it but he wearied of whispering "Norbury" in Holmes's ear so often.

Everything Holmes gleaned from said watch fit Watson's father; the drunkenness, the poverty, and the occasional short intervals of prosperity. It is true that the elder Watson gambled away his fortune, drank to the limits of moderation, and haunted pawn-shops for the better part of his life.

Australian pawn- shop owners followed the practice of their ilk in England by scratching dates on the inside of the watch instead of handing out tickets. So this is how Watson came to maturity Down Under, how he saved his good friend, Sherlock Holmes from embarrassment, and how the real story on his father's watch came to be known.

Cooey

Searching for God in the Canon

Through an extensive, non-computer search of Baring-Gould's "Annotated Sherlock Holmes," I discovered that "God," or "Lord," or "Jove," are mentioned in all but 5 cases in the Canon. The exceptions are: ENGR, RETI, SILV, FINA, AND NOBL. ("Lord" St. Simon does not count). ABBE originally appeared on this list, but in the last paragraph, Holmes says, "Vox populi, vox Dei," and so, there we have "God" in Latin.

The deity appears in REDC in Italian when Emilia Lucca shouts, "Oh, Dio Mio, you have killed him," and in GREE, Sophy Kratides moans, "Oh, my God, it is Paul," and Mr. Melas explains that "these words were spoken in Greek."

The word "God" appears some 150 times in the Canon; "Lord," we see 33 times, and "Jove," 20 times. Whereas "Jesus" is never spoken, "Christ," is mentioned thrice. In SIGN, Major Sholto yelled, in a voice which Thaddeus could never forget, "Keep him out! For Christ's sake, keep him out." In VALL, John McMurdo cried, "By the Cross of Christ, I swear it," and in BLUE, James Ryder whines, "Oh don't bring it into court! For Christ's sake, don't."

Holmes used "Jove" more than anyone else (CHAS, HOUN, 3STU, IDEN, PRIO, MISS (twice), REDC, BLUE, BRUC (twice), LION, AND WIST). Others who say "Jove" are: Reginald Musgrave (MUSG), Lestrade (SIXN), Hall Pycroft

(STOC), Watson (STUD), Inspector Bardle (LION), and Colonel Hayter (REIG), who uses it twice.

VALL is the winner of the search with a combination of 28 (19 "God," 9 "Lord"); STUD places, with 16 (11 "God," 4 "Lord," 1 "Jove"), and HOUN shows, with 13 (12 "God," 1 "Jove").

When I presented this data to Irv Kamil, of Mrs. Hudson's Cliff Dwellers, he disputed it. His calculations, done in a computer word search, came up with totally different figures. After a paragraph by paragraph investigation we concluded that his copy of the Canon (Doubleday) was far different than mine (Baring Gould).

God save the Queen.

Knocks and Boosts

My junior high school yearbook had comments after each graduate's name, with either praise or mockery. This was referred to as Knocks or Boosts. Next to my name was "Let's build him over, there's a screw loose." One other read: "Before, of Before and After;" my favorite was "Tarzan - - of the Pygmies."

To Sherlock Holmes she would always be the woman, which was high praise from the Master for Irene Adler. But how did Canonical characters view Sherlock Holmes? With awe or scorn? Were their comments pejorative or praiseworthy? Were they impressed with his unique abilities or were they unimpressed? Were any of them objective? How did they see him?

Let us now count the ways. But, for this exercise we shall excuse Dr. Watson.

We'll get to his observations on another occasion. And just for now we will offer praise and objectivity, later we will inspect scorn, anger and indifference.

Praise

"I don't know how you manage this, Mr. Holmes, but it seems to me that all the detectives of fact and fancy would be children in your hands. That's your line of life, sir, and you may take the word of a man who has seen something of the world." Trevor Sr. (GLOR)

"But I understand Holmes, that you are turning to practical ends those powers with which you used to amaze us?"

Reginald Musgrave (MUSG)

"If you are unable to come I shall give you fuller details, and would esteem it a great kindness if you would favor me with your opinions."

Tobias Gregson (STUD)

"You will appreciate that, Mr. Sherlock Holmes, for we are both brain-workers."

Tobias Gregson (STUD)

"Well, Mr. Holmes, it is difficult for me to refuse you anything, for you have been of use to the force once or twice in the past, and we owe you a good turn at Scotland Yard."

Inspector Lestrade (NORW)

"Well...I've seen you handle a good many cases, Mr. Holmes, but I don't know that I ever knew a more workmanlike one than that. We're not jealous of you at Scotland Yard. No sir, we're very proud of you, and if you come down tomorrow, there's not a man from the oldest inspector to the youngest constable, who wouldn't be glad to shake you by the hand."

Lestrade (SIXN)

"I have ordered a carriage...I knew your energetic nature, and that you would not be happy until you had been on the scene of the crime."

Lestrade (BOSC)

"We all three shook hands, and I saw at once from the reverential way in which Lestrade gazed at my companion that he had learned a good deal since the days when they had first worked together."

Watson (HOUN)

"You would have made an actor and a rare one."

Athelney Jones (SIGN)

"Twice already in his career had Holmes helped him to attain success, his own sole reward being the intellectual joy of the problem. For this reason the affection and respect of the Scotchman for his amateur colleague were profound, and he showed them by the frankness with which he consulted Holmes in every difficulty. Mediocrity knows nothing higher than itself; but talent instantly recognizes genius, and MacDonald had talent enough for his profession to enable him to perceive that there was no humiliation in seeking the assistance of one who had already stood alone in Europe, both in his gifts and in his experience."

Watson (VALL)

"I recognized him at once as Stanley Hopkins, a young police inspector, for whose future Holmes had high hopes, while he in turn professed the admiration and respect of a pupil for the scientific methods of the famous amateur.

Watson (BLAC)

"It seems to me that I have been making a fool of myself from the beginning. I understand now, what I should never have forgotten, that I am the pupil and you are the master. Even now I see what you have done, but I don't know how you did it or what it signifies."

Stanley Hopkins (BLAC)

"You really did it very well. You took me in completely."

Irene Adler (SCAN)

"I am immensely indebted to you."

The King of Bohemia (SCAN)

"Oh, indeed. You seem to have done the thing very completely. I must compliment you."

John Clay (REDH)

"Really, Mr. Holmes… I do not know how the bank can thank you or repay you. There is no doubt that you have detected and defeated in the most complete manner one of the most determined attempts at bank robbery that have ever come within my experience."

Mr. Merryweather (REDH)

"I only know Mr. Holmes through some business dealings which we have had, but I have every respect for his talents and his character."

Culverton Smith (DYIN)

"We can only regard it as a special Providence that you should chance to be here at the time, for in all of England you are the one man we need."

Mr. Roundhay (DEVI)

"A savior, able to solve any problem and could never be beaten."

The opinion of Major Prendergast (FIVE)

"But he [Fairdale Hobbs] would never cease talking of it – your kindness, sir, and the way in which you brought light into the darkness."

Mrs. Warren (REDC)

"Lord Backwater tells me that I may place implicit reliance upon your judgment and discretion."
Lord Robert St. Simon (NOBL)

"There is no getting past you, Mr. Holmes. Wonderful

"Sir James Damery (ILLU)

"You clever, clever fiend… You cunning cunning fiend."

Colonel Sebastian Moran (EMPT)

Objectivity

"You interest me very much Mr. Holmes. I had hardly expected so dolichocephalic a skull or such well-marked supra-orbital development."

Dr. Mortimer (HOUN)

"You have less frontal development than I should have expected."

Professor Moriarty (FINA)

"Holmes is a little too scientific for my tastes - it approaches cold bloodedness. I could imagine his giving a friend a little pinch of the latest vegetable alkaloid, not out of malevolence, you understand, but simply out of a spirit of inquiry in order to have an accurate idea of the effects. To do him justice, I think that he would take it himself with the same readiness. He appears to have a passion for definite and exact knowledge."

Stamford (STUD)

Those were the Boosts. Stay tuned for the Knocks.

Knocks

From Those Who Show Scorn; Those Who Are Angry And Those Who Are Very Unimpressed.

Scorn

Gregson and Lestrade had watched the manoeuvres of their amateur companion with considerable curiosity and some contempt. (STUD)

"Excuse my amusement, Mr. Holmes," said he, "but it is really funny to see you trying to play a hand with no cards in it. I don't think anyone could do it better, but it is rather pathetic, all the same. Not a color card there, Mr. Holmes, nothing but the smallest of the small."

Baron Gruner (ILLU)

"Now then, Mr. Cocksure," said the salesman, "I thought that I was out of geese, but before I finish you'll find that there is still one left in my shop."

Breckinridge (BLUE)

"Yes, some of us are a little too much inclined to be cock-sure, Mr. Holmes."

Inspector Lestrade (NORW)

"Still at it, then?" said he to Holmes. "I thought you Londoners were never at fault. You don't seem to be so very quick, after all."

Alec Cunningham (REIG)

Anger

"...I am aware of your profession – one of which I by no means approve...Where your calling is more open to criticism is when you pry into the secrets of private individuals, when you rake up family matters which are better hidden, and when you incidentally waste the time of men who are more busy than yourself."

Dr. Leslie Armstrong (MISS)

"You can lie as you like, Holmes. My word is always as good as yours."

Culverton Smith (DYIN)

"You thieves! Spies and thieves!" (Watson included). I have caught you, have I? You are in my power. I'll serve you!"

Jethro Rucastle (COPP)

"Speak out man! You can't sit there and play with me like a cat with a mouse."

Jack Crocker (ABBE)

"You are an impudent fellow! Do you mean to say that my mistress has told a lie?"

Theresa Wright (ABBE)

"Mr. Holmes... This is surely most unfair and ungenerous upon your part."

"You - you insult me, Mr. Holmes."

"You are trying to frighten me. It is not a very manly thing, Mr. Holmes, to come here and browbeat a woman"

"You are mad, Mr. Holmes – you are mad!"

"I tell you again, Mr. Holmes, that you are under some absurd illusion."

Lady Trelawney Hope (SECO)

"Lie number one," said the old man; "I never saw either of them until two months ago, and I have never been in Africa in my life, so you can put that in your pipe and smoke it, Mr. Busybody Holmes!"

Mr. Williamson (SOLI)

"You are making fools of us, Mr. Holmes!"

"And how long have you been playing this trick upon us, Mr. Holmes?" said the inspector angrily. "How long have you allowed us to waste ourselves upon a search you knew to be an absurd one?"

Alec MacDonald (VALL)

"I know you, you scoundrel! I have heard of you before. You are Holmes, the meddler. Holmes, the busybody! Holmes, the Scotland Yard Jack-in-office!"

Dr. Grimesby Roylott (SPEC)

"Why you are a common burglar."

"Ah, you've blundered badly for once Mr. Sherlock Holmes."

Holy Peters (LADY)

"Upon my word, you are getting on" said he. "Do all your successes depend upon this prodigious power of bluff?"

Dr. Leon Sterndale (DEVI)

"You are a private individual. You have no warrant for my arrest. The whole proceeding is absolutely illegal and outrageous."

Von Bork (LAST)

"Ralph," he said, "telephone down to the county police and ask the inspector to send up two constables. Tell him there are burglars in the house." (said to Holmes and James M. Dodd)

Colonel Emsworth (BLAN)

"See here, Masser Holmes, you keep your hands out of other folks' business. Leave folks to manage their own affairs. Got that, Masser Holmes?"

Steve Dixie (3GAB)

"What is this intrusion and this insulting message?"

Isadora Klein (3GAB)

"What the devil do you mean by this, Mr. Holmes? Do you dismiss my case?"

"Plain enough, but what's at the back of it? Raising the price on me, or afraid to tackle it, or what? I've a right to a plain answer."

J. Neil Gibson (THOR)

"That is conclusive" said the professor, glaring angrily at my companion. "Now, sir" - he leaned forward with his two hands upon the table - "it seems to me that your position is a very questionable one."

Professor Presbury (CREE)

"You are mad!" he cried. "You are talking insanely."

Professor Sergius Coram (GOLD)

"Who the devil are you?" he thundered. "And what are you doing upon my property... Do you hear me?" he cried. "Who are you? What are you doing here?" His cudgel quivered in the air.

Sir Robert Norburton (SHOS)

"Leave me alone! What are you a-doin'of?" she screeched.

"Who be you, anyhow, and what right have you a-pullin' me about like this?"

"I'll see you in hell first."

Susan Stockdale (3GAB)

The nobleman's reply was interrupted by his secretary, who broke in with some heat. "His Grace is not in the habit of posting letters himself," said he.

James Wilder (PRIO)

Unimpressed

"It's Mr. Sherlock Holmes, the theorist…It's true you set us on the right track; but you'll own now that it was more by good luck than good guidance."

Athelney Jones (SIGN)

"Mr. Holmes, Mr. Holmes," he said "I have been expecting you to do something original. This has been done so often, and what good has ever come from it?"

Charles Augustus Milverton (CHAS)

"For a moment I thought you had done something clever."

Joseph Harrison (NAVA)

"Well, I never," said he. "I thought at first that you had done something clever, but I see that there was nothing in it, after all."

Jabez Wilson (REDH)

Why, Mr. Holmes I thought you knew things."

Cyril Overton (MISS)

Initial Offerings

Once again, a comment at the Epilogues Scion meeting, in Chatham, N.J., has offered a subject for a monograph, this time on Canonical initials. And there are a host of them, many that were essential in solving a case. For instance: J.H.N, C.P.R, and P.C., in BLAC; L.L. in HOUN; V.V. and P-E-N, comprised of a Big P with a flourish above it, e and n smaller, in VALL; E.J.D. and J.H. in STUD; K.K.K. in FIVE, F.H.M. in NOBL, and J.A. in GLOR. J.H.N refers to the unfortunate John Hopley Neligan; C.P.R. is not just a means of resuscitation, but also, the Canadian Pacific Railway, and P.C. could be Peter Carey or Patrick Cairns, or even Paul Churchill. L.L. is Laura Lyons, daughter of the most litigious citizen of Dartmoor, and V.V., of course, is our famous Valley of Fear, Vermissa by name, while P.e.n. stands for the Pennsylvania Small Arms Company.

E.J.D. and J.H. stand for the two antagonists from Utah, Enoch J. Drebber, and Jefferson Hope (who is in Europe). K.K.K. we are all familiar with as the infamous Ku Klux Klan, of post-Civil War terror, and Francis Hay Moulton's identity was needed in solving the disappearance of the West Coast heiress, Hatty Doran. But what about the other F.M., Flora Millar? Didn't she have a middle initial? We just don't know. But there is even another F.M. in LION, Fitzroy McPherson, one of Cyanea Capillata's victims, J.A., tattooed in the bend of senior Trevor's elbow does him in as Sherlock Holmes unravels part of the J.P.'s past by reading this decades-old inscription.

These are the best known initials but there are a host of others. H.W., on the back of Watson's watch, offers Holmes a magnificent opportunity to show his amazing powers of observation, and awe poor Watson (SIGN). What about the letter "S," so important in CARD? Did it stand for Susan or Sarah? And the initials that make Holmes almost queasy, C.A.M., referring to the worst man in London, the reptilian Charles Augustus Milverton (CHAS). We have two J.P.s, Justices of the Peace, in the Senior Trevor (GLOR) and Cunningham (REIG) and Holmes leaves an envelope with some pips inside for Captain Calhoun, of the Lone Star, and signs it, S.H. for J.O. (Sherlock Holmes, for John Openshaw, FIVE). The most complicated set of initials shows up in SCAN, where it appears on notepaper received from Count Von Kramm. A large "E", with a small "g", a "P" and a large "G" with a small "t" woven into the texture of the paper, all of which meant Gesellschaft Papier Egria, a paper company from Egria, in, you know it, Bohemia.

The most unusual initials appear when Holmes proceeds to adorn the wall opposite his armchair with a patriotic V.R. done in bullet-pocks (MUSG). And Holmes's initials show up when he commands Watson in unforgettable, laconic, almost comical fashion, "Come at once if convenient – if inconvenient come all the same. S.H. (CREE).

Some of our initials stand for academic or national achievements, such as D.D. (Doctor of Divinity) for Elias Whitney (TWIS); M.A., Ph.D., plus (master of arts; Doctor of Philosophy), for Thorneycroft Huxtable (PRIO); C.B.

(Companion of the Bath) for Sir Augustus Moran (EMPT), dad of the sharpshooting Colonel Sebastian Moran; V.C. (Victoria Cross) for the cranky Colonel Emsworth (BLAN), K.G. (Knight of the Garter) and P.C. (Privy Councilor) just two of the many honors heaped upon Lord Holdernesse (PRIO), M.R.C.S. (Member of the Royal College of Surgeons) which, apparently, was not enough to allow the good Dr. Mortimer to call himself Doctor, except as a courtesy, something baffling to Americans (HOUN), and D.M.A.O.F, part of the signature of J. W. Windle, one of the more charming Scowrers, of Merton County Lodge 249. Windle was a powerful Division Master of the Ancient Order of Freemen (VALL).

These are not all of the Canonical initials by far, but they will suffice. Well, not quite. There is one more that is the most tantalizing of all, and the subject of much guesswork. That is the "G" in G. Lestrade. Is it George, Geronimo, Gipper? Could it be Glengary, Gilligan? Could be, but, alas, we shall never know.

Thank you,

E.A. Livingston, B.A., M.A., A.A.S.

In the Eye of the Beholder

I count 83 different women mentioned in the Canon, from the 90-year-old Rose Spender, of senile decay (LADY), to 14-year-old Patience Moran (BOSC), the flower-picking reluctant eavesdropper. Some are described by Dr. Watson (or Holmes) in minute detail; some are merely mentioned. Out of the 83 there are 14 who are beautiful, almost 17 per cent. Imagine if 17 per cent of our female population was beautiful? Out of the approximately 160 million women in the United States, some 27 million would be beauties. Does that sound plausible or are English women just more beautiful than ours? I recall a scene from a Peter Sellers movie where he plays a very long haired adulterer. Sellers' distraught wife accosts him and says, "Tell me. Is she more beautiful than me?" Sellers looks at her with disbelief and answers, "Is she more beautiful than you? I'm more beautiful than you!"

Sadly, of our 14 Canonical beauties, two are dead. Lets us deal with the deceased first. Mrs. Godfrey Staunton was young and beautiful but she was a goner (MISS), and Brenda Tregannis had been a very beautiful girl but, again, she was not among the living (DEVI). Nancy Barclay was a woman of great beauty (CROO) and of Lady Brackenstall, Watson wrote, "seldom have I seen so graceful a figure, so womanly a presence, and so beautiful a face" (ABBE). The much sought after Lady Francis Carfax was a beautiful woman, still in fresh middle age (LADY), and Ivy Douglas is described as a beautiful woman, tall, dark and slender, some twenty years younger than her husband. John Douglas' first wife, Etta Shafter, was also "a very beautiful woman" (VALL).

Near the Thor Bridge we have two beauties, one a suicide, and the other, a framed murderess. I refer, of course, to Maria Pinto and Grace Dunbar. Maria was even rare and wonderful in her beauty, at least sayeth our Abraham Lincoln keyed to base uses, J. Neil Gibson (THOR). Maria came from Brazil; our next beauty is from Costa Rica: Beryl Garcia Stapleton, who is not only a beauty but who has beautiful, dark, eager eyes. Have you ever seen eager eyes?

One young lady, whose voice is like a wind from an iceberg, Violet De Merville, is beautiful but with the ethereal other-world beauty of some fanatic whose thoughts were set on high, and our only dazzler from Kings County, that is Brooklyn, Emilia Lucca, is a tall and beautiful woman (REDC). Lady Trelawney Hope, of the copied key, is the beautiful youngest daughter of the Duke of Belminster. Our last entry, Violet Smith, is a young and beautiful solitary cyclist (SOLI). This is, however, not the end of the parade of good-looking Canonical women. Just because you are not beautiful does not mean that you can't still be pretty attractive. Here we have Alice Morphy (CREE) who is a very perfect girl both in mind and body; Annie Harrison (NAVA) who is striking looking; Alice Turner (BOSC), who Doctor Watson thought one of the most lovely young women that he had ever seen in his life; Alice Carpentier (STUD), an uncommonly fine girl; and Lucy Ferrier, the flower of Utah (STUD). And just one more. Isadora Klein, of the sugar

Kleins, was tall and queenly, with a perfect figure and two wonderful Spanish eyes, eyes that Dr. Watson said, looked murder at us both.

Drink, Drank, Drunk

There are ten certifiable drunkards in the Canon, and one who was crying drunk, but a wonderful fake. One drunkard has no name, only initials; three have surnames only; but the rest we can identify rather easily. Watson's unhappy elder brother, known to us only as H.W., leads off (SIGN), followed by Hudson (GLOR), Mr. Norlett (SHOS), and Toller (COPP). Following, in alphabetical order are: Eustace Brackenstall (ABBE), Jim Browner (CARD), Peter Carey (BLAC), Enoch Drebber (STUD), Mrs. Tangey (NAVA), and Roaring Jack Woodley (SOLI). Jefferson Hope, of course, did the imitation that fooled Constable John Rance (STUD).

Three Canonical characters do get drunk (two under great stress), but this is not their normal condition: Baron Gruner (a bit drunk, ILLU), the elder Trevor (dead drunk, GLOR), and Elias Openshaw (in a sort of a drunken frenzy, FIVE). In twelve cases brandy is administered as a stimulant: to Julia Stoner (SPEC), Sir Henry and Beryl Stapleton (HOUN), Bannister (3STU), Ian Murdoch and J.G. Wood (LION), James Ryder (BLUE), Thorneycroft Huxtable (PRIO), Percy Phelps (NAVA), Holmes (REIG), Watson (EMPT), Victor Hatherley (with water, ENGR), John Scott Eccles (with soda, WIST) and Mr. Melas (with ammonia, GREE). Elias Openshaw (FIVE), Trevor Sr. (GLOR) and most likely Hudson (GLOR), got drunk on brandy, and in two instances (BLAC, SECO) brandy is mentioned, but it is not imbibed.

The favorite Canonical drink, surprisingly enough, is coffee, which we find in fifteen cases (STUD, SCAN, REDH, FIVE, BRUC, BERY, MUSG, REIG, NAVA, SPEC, GOLD, HOUN, WIST, ILLU, BLAC); tea is in seven (BERY, CROO, RESI, ABBE, LION, SUSS, BOSC); water in six (NORW, GOLD, MISS, STUD, SILV, DYIN); and milk in three. Thorneycroft Huxtable has milk and a biscuit in order to regain his equilibrium (PRIO); Holmes uses milk to test the poisoned capsules (STUD); and our thirsty swamp adder allegedly swigged milk during his rigorous training program (SPEC).

Whisky is mentioned in BLAC, NOBL, SIGN, STUD, VALL and REDH, and taken, sometimes neat, sometimes with soda, or water. More people partake of this aqua vitae in VALL than in any other case, where it is set up on no less than six occasions.

Beer drinking appears in only three stories: BLUE, SOLI and SCAN. In the first it leads to conversation with the bar owner; in the second to Holmes's failure to entirely avoid a vicious backhander from a slogging ruffian, and in the third to wash down some cold beef.

Other spirits mentioned, although only in one case each, are rum (BLAC), half-and-half (SCAN), and curacao (BRUC).

Wine appears in seven cases in its generic form, but it is mostly cited and not sipped. In ABBE the dregs from wine lead to a Sherlockian deduction; in SHOS, Josiah Barnes, landlord of the Green Dragon, drinks his own wine (at least that is what Holmes implies); James Windibank is a traveller in wines (IDEN); Vamberry is a wine merchant (MUSG); and Mrs. Toller is locked in the wine cellar (COPP). In STUD Stamford looks over his wineglass at his old friend, Watson; in TWIS, Mrs. Watson offers her old schoolmate companion, Kate Whitney, some wine and water, and in SILV we hear of spirits of wine, which is not wine at all, but alcohol, to wash Silver Blaze's face and leg. Special wines mentioned include: Champagne (VALL), Beaune, Chianti, Tokay, (SIGN), Claret (CARD, DYIN), Comet Wine (only from years of notable comets, STOC), Montrachet (VEIL), Port (CREE, GLOR, SIGN) and Sherry (GLOR, NOBL). The eight pence sherry led Holmes to discover Francis Hay Moulton's hotel (NOBL). Although we don't know exactly what is in the group of ancient and cobwebby bottles Holmes bought to celebrate the reunion of Mr. and Mrs. Francis Hay Moulton (NOBL), we do know how special the wine is that the two old friends drink over Von Bork's slumbering body (LAST). It is Imperial Tokay, from Emperor Franz Joseph's special cellar at the Schoenbrunn Palace.

Who could whine about that?

It's a Dog's Life

Some time ago, Peter McIntyre discussed the dreadful fate of Canonical ships, the Gloria Scott, the Lone Star, and others. After that talk I received a phone call from the A.S.P.C.A. requesting equal time for members of the canine persuasion. It seems obviously true that a pack of Canonical dogs really had a bad Canonical time, just as bad, if not worse, than those ships.

Let us take the case of Carlo the first, Carlo the second, Roy, and a bunch of other dog-faces that don't even warrant names. Sir Eustace Brackenstall drenched Mary Fraser from Adelaide's dog with petroleum and set it afire (ABBE). Fitzroy McPherson's little dog is thrown through a plate glass window by Ian Murdoch (LION). Dr. Mortimer's curly haired spaniel was devoured by the Hound (leaving only a skeleton and a tangle of brown hair) and that phosphorescent S.O.B., in turn, is shot by Holmes, Watson and Lestrade (HOUN). A three-weapon problem. Then there are the two Carlos. One is pumped full of curare by Jacky Ferguson, as an experiment (SUSS), and poor Carlo's hind legs move irregularly, its tail on the ground. And he is not the only Canonical pup to be poisoned. In SCAN, when Holmes gets hold of Jefferson Hope's translucent pills, he asks Watson to fetch that poor little devil of a terrier which has been bad so long and which the landlady wanted to put out of its pain. And Holmes, after one nerve-wracking failure, does just this, an example of canine euthanasia. Carlos II, the mastiff, is fed only once a day and not that much then (COPP), and winds up taking a bite of Jephro Rucastle's throat. And since we're on the dog food topic, Trevor, Jr. apparently didn't feed his bull terrier that frequently, either, as one morning at school, while Holmes went down to chapel it tried his ankle for a snack. (GLOR).

Let us now talk about Roy, Professor Presbury's great wolfhound. When the professor goes ape he monkeys around with poor Roy by throwing pebbles in his face, prodding him with a stick, and maddening the poor thing (CREE), and all Carlo can do is howl, "I'm nothin' but an old hound dog." The famous Shoscombe spaniel has to be given away since its mistress has gone to the great beyond. It flies into a furious rage on approaching Mr. Norlett, masquerading as Lady Beatrice Falder. What a cruel hoax. As Holmes comments, dogs don't make mistakes (SHOS).

Holmes maintains that happy dogs live in happy families (CREE). Ergo; unhappy dogs…well, you get it. Can you imagine what kind of families these pups came from? There may be other Canonical canines who also suffered but let us let sleeping dogs lie. You must admit, however, that Canonical ships are not the only entity to get a raw deal.

In closing, I would like to quote one of the most famous of all American dogs, Little Orphan Annie's Sandy. This quote comes directly from page 1126 of Bartlett's Familiar Quotations.

Arf. Arf.

Giving the Devil his Due

The word "devil" has a host of meanings and between talking directly about the Devil himself, and the use of devilish adjectives, there are over seventy Canonical references, in twenty-seven cases, to that most famous fallen angel.

Leading off, and used frequently, is this: a person, usually one in unfortunate or pitiable circumstances - the poor devil. Stamford commiserates thusly after hearing of Watson's misfortunes in Afghanistan (STUD); John Douglas, believe it or not, calls his dead arch-enemy, Ted Baldwin, "a poor devil," and his alter ego, John McMurdo, snarls to Boss McGinty about "the poor devils of men and women that you held under your grip" (VALL). Dr Watson takes one look at his "dying" detective friend and calls him "a poor devil" (DYIN), and Holmes, talking of Ronder, the circus owner, mistakenly thinks that "poor devil" might have helped Eugenia escape from the lion's claws. Eugenia Ronder says that her husband was "the devil who tormented me," calls her favorite clown, Jimmy Griggs "a poor devil" (VEIL), and Holmes refers to "the poor devils done to death in the Bar of Gold (TWIS). Finally, Altamount says that Steiner, a German spy, "is a poor devil" who will be lucky to get off with his life (LAST).

Then we have the person of great cleverness, energy or recklessness - like "the cunning devils" who murdered John Openshaw (FIVE), the devilish cunning of Stapleton (HOUN), and "the cunning devil," Baron Gruner (ILLU). Leon Sterndale says "I believe that you are the devil himself," in complimenting Holmes on his shadowing ability (DEVI), and Watson describes Sir Robert Norberton, as "about the most daredevil rider in England," and "a devil of a fellow" (SHOS). Holmes laments the fact that the <u>Aurora</u> is "going like the devil" (SIGN); and Von Bork is described as a "devil-may-care young fellow" (LAST). And where the devil connotes hellish damnation we have Mr. Roundhay crying that his "parish is devil-ridden," and that "Satan himself is loose in it" (DEVI). Of course, the devil's- foot root itself is hellishly damnable, too. We also have adjectives and nouns that spring from the Devil. Jim Browner refers to "devilry on the part of this woman" {Sarah} and adds that his wife, Mary, "saw the devil's light in his eyes" (CARD). Holmes uses "devilry" to describe an unsigned, enigmatic note in his letter box (VALL), and again, after looking through the keyhole at the dead, grinning face of Bartholomew Sholto, he utters, "there is something devilish in this, Watson" (SIGN). Mortimer Tregennis calls his siblings' deaths "devilish" (DEVI), and Holmes puzzles over what "devilish device" Josiah Amberley used to decoy his wife and Ray Ernest to their deaths (RETI). Holmes sends "their own devilish trademark," to Captain James Calhoun, of the <u>Lone Star</u> (FIVE), and Von Bork and Von Herling admit to having "stirred up such a devil's brew of Irish Civil War" (LAST). Hugo Baskerville's painting shows "a lurking devil in his eyes" (HOUN); Boss McGinty wants to fix "the old devil Morris," and the Scowrer's treasurer refers to "the old devil Archie Swindon" (VALL). Holmes says, "But what, in the name of the devil!" when Grimesby Roylott suddenly appears at Baker Street (SPEC); Watson can't believe that honest Bob Ferguson's wife casts him "in the character of fiend or devil" (SUSS), and Elias Openshaw "was not be cooped up, like a sheep in a pen, by man or devil" (FIVE). Holmes also says that "the devil knows best what he said," referring to Sir George Burnwell's spell over Mary Holder (BERY), and Breckinridge angrily announces that "I wish you were all at the devil together" after being pestered by a gaggle of goose-seekers at Covent Garden Market (BLUE). A number of characters ejaculate the devil's name. J. Neil Gibson says, "what the devil do you mean by this?" when Holmes dismisses first his case and then him (THOR). Holy Peters shouts, "What the devil do you mean?" (LADY); Cecil Barker cries, "What the devil is the meaning of all this?" (VALL); Sir Robert Norberton shouts at Holmes "Who the devil are you?" (SHOS), and Colonel Emsworth yells at his servant, Ralph, "What the devil are you waiting for?" (BLAN). McMurdo roars at Teddy Marvin, "what the devil do you mean by that?" and when Jacob Shafter mentions Ted Baldwin, he adds hotly, "And who the devil is he?" (VALL).

Harmless items include Holmes's self-description as being "the most incurably lazy devil," and he tests Jefferson Hope's poison on "that poor little devil of a terrier," (STUD). Angry evocations of the Devil are the most damning. Emilia Lucca says, "He is a devil and a monster, meaning Black Gorgiano (REDC); Kitty Winter says, "You surely know enough about this devil," and Baron Gruner pays back the compliment by gasping out "oh, the she-devil!," (ILLU). Jonathan Small welts the "little devil,"

Tonga; and refers to "200,000 black devils let loose," referring to India (SIGN). John Douglas says of the Scowrers that "these devils would give me no rest," while Cecil Barker asks Holmes, "Do you say no one can ever get level at this king-devil?" (VALL). When we describe the Devil as the supreme spirit of evil, we have Mrs. Bob Ferguson calling little Jackie "a fiend and a devil" (SUSS); John Turner describing Charles McCarthy as a devil incarnate (BOSC); and Trevor referring to Hudson as the Devil (GLOR). The ancient manuscript detailing the legend of the Hound says that "Hugo became as one who hath a devil" (HOUN), and Holmes says that "to take on the Father of Evil himself would, perhaps, be too ambitious a task." Later, he adds, "If the Devil did desire to have a hand in the affairs of men," and "the Devil's agents may be of flesh and blood, may they not?" In addition, he wonders about a devil "with merely local powers" (DEVI). He also feels that Charles Augustus Milverton is as cunning as the Evil One (CHAS). Poor policeman Walters. He takes the cake. He is the only Canonical character who thought he really saw the Devil in person. No pity for him from Inspector Baynes, though, who expected that even if the Devil appeared a constable on duty should never thank God that he could not lay his hands on him (WIST).

You must admit that would be a Hell of a situation.

A Case of Identity

Some of us recall old Abrahams who was in such mortal terror of his life (LADY). And some may remember Augusto Barelli, Emilia Lucca's father (REDC). But how many of us are acquainted with Baron Beverley? Or the Earl of Carston, or even the Lord Lieutenant of Hallamshire? Actually, they are all the same guy. Sorry, your grace. I mean the same lord. Holdernesse is his name and those were just a few of his titles (PRIO).

And here are some more noblemen who seem unfamiliar. Do you remember the Earl of Dovercourt? Lady Eva Blackwell planned on marrying him (CHAS). How about Lord Merrow and Sir Charles Hardy? Merrow's letter and Hardy's report were in Trelawney Hope's famous dispatch box (SECO).

Lord Harringly and Sir George Folliot were neighbors of Aloysius Garcia of Wisteria Lodge (WIST). For the record, Harringby lived at The Dingle. And in this same case, how about Eckermann? Eckermann? He wrote <u>Voodoism and the Negroid Religions</u>.

How many of us remember Archie Swindon, Van Deher, Van Shorst, and Chester Wilcox? They all earned the enmity of the Scowrers in Vermissa Valley and they were beaten up, killed, or forced to flee for their lives (VALL).

Who was Bob? Who was Poncho? The former was Lucy

Ferrier's brother who didn't survive the trek West and the latter was her mustang, whose skittishness led to her being saved from stampeding steers by our favorite avenger, Jefferson Hope (STUD).

Who was Jacobs, who was Stephens? These chaps were butlers for Trelawney Hope (SECO) and Lady Beatrice Falder (SHOS) respectively. Here are a couple of easy ones; Price and Harris. They were the aliases of Watson and Holmes in their job interview with Harry Pinner. Poor Watson, reduced to being a clerk. Disgraceful. At least Holmes took on the guise of an accountant (STOC).

And then there are the lesser-known policemen. Sargeant Tuson and Constable Pollock, who arrested Beddington in STOC; Algar of the Liverpool force (CARD), Hunt, the Vermissa Valley officer who tried to take in a Scowrer and was murdered for his efforts (VALL); Harry Murcher, the London constable on the Holland Grove beat (STUD); and Edmunds, of the Barkshire constabulary, who was involved in the Abba Parvas tragedy (VEIL).

Slide rule accuracy indicates that there are at least forty other lesser-known Canonical characters. But who's counting? I'll save them for another paper.

Henry Ward Beecher

The Montague Street Lodgers, who meet on Montague Street, in Brooklyn, toast the only Canonical Brooklynites, Gennaro and Emilia Lucca (REDC). But there is another Brooklynite mentioned in the Canon who was as famous in his day as anyone since and his unframed portrait hung on the wall at 221B Baker Street (CARD). I refer to Henry Ward Beecher.

But who was he and what did he do?

Connecticut's most celebrated minister, Lyman Beecher, raised two children who would leave indelible marks on America during the Civil War era. His daughter, Harriet Beecher Stowe, wrote the most popular and controversial book of the day, Uncle Tom's Cabin, and his son Henry, became Brooklyn's - and the country's - most illustrious preacher.

The thirty-three-year old Henry Ward Beecher became the spiritual leader of the pioneer Congregationalist Plymouth church in Brooklyn in 1847. Neither the church nor the city would ever be the same again. His extraordinary sermons drew such unprecedented crowds, including many who flocked from New York on the Fulton Street Ferry (dubbed "Beecher's Ferry"), that his new church could not accommodate them all. When it burned down in 1849 a new and more spacious edifice rose in its place on Orange Street near Hicks. No distinguished visitor ever left New York without being treated to a Beecher sermon.

Beecher spiced everyday language with local slang and laced his homilies with humor, unusual for a preacher of his day. His sermons covered a range of subjects: temperance, suffrage, reform, phrenology, slavery, anti-slavery, and the impending war. His style of presentation seemed like normal conversation and his ability to communicate established a strong empathy with churchgoers without being authoritarian. One listener compared Beecher's technique with that of Edward Everett, the leading orator of the day, the main speaker who preceded Abraham Lincoln at Gettysburg in November 1863. Everett, he said, reminded him of a "peacefully flowing river in which was reflected the beautiful images of the flowers and foliage upon its banks." Beecher's style, however, resembled that of "a mountain torrent rushing wildly along carrying everything before it by its very impetuosity and force."

Beecher also presided over a highly efficient organization. Even though as many as 1500 worshippers might attend a single service, his eight deacons, performing the sacrament each communion day, distributed bread and wine to all in less than ten minutes.

Plymouth Church members, many originally from New England, grew in numbers from twenty-three in 1847 to 343 in 1850. Seven years later 1,200 Congregationalists claimed membership, with a waiting list of more than 2,000. As the largest public hall in Brooklyn, the church served also as an important meeting place. Over the years it featured such famous speakers as William Makepeace Thackeray, Charles Dickens, Ralph Waldo Emerson, Josh Billings, and Artemis Ward. The

church also served as a pulpit for anti- slavery advocates --
Wendell Phillips, William Lloyd Garrison, John Greenleaf
Whittier, Charles Sumner -- yet Beecher himself was not
enamored with their methods. In particular he found Garrison's
"screaming" undignified, futile, and counterproductive. Any
mind-change concerning slavery, he felt, would come through
moderate, Beecher-like persuasion, something that,
unfortunately, vanished overnight with his involvement in the
aftermath of the Kansas-Nebraska Act.

That legislation, passed in 1854 and based on Illinois Senator
Stephen A. Douglas's concept of popular sovereignty, mandated
that both Kansas and Nebraska be organized into territories on
the basis of an election to determine the status of slavery. As
settlers rushed westward to take up residence and to cast their
votes, Kansas became a bloody battleground of rival factions.
The soon-to-be infamous John Brown and his sons hacked to
death pro-slavery men at Pottawatamie in the "name of
freedom," and Missouri "border ruffians" plundered Lawrence,
Kansas, "for slavery." The civil warfare in Kansas, although
contained in 1859, continued sporadically for the next two years,
greatly heightening the tension between the North and South
that caused the Civil War.

Beecher involved himself inadvertently in the slavery fray while
attending a meeting in New Haven, Connecticut, on March 22,
1856. He learned that a contingent of New Englanders was
heading west to settle in Kansas to vote for an anti-slavery
ticket. They needed weapons for protection, and in the heat of
the moment Beecher rashly pledged the Plymouth Church to

supply twenty-five rifles to promote a "just solution" of the western problems. His gesture became an acute embarrassment. The press singled him out as a radical, based solely on this newly acquired fame. Beecher's contribution to the abolitionist cause to that point had been minor, yet the promised weapons suddenly become "Beecher's Bibles" and his bailiwick the "Church of the Holy Rifles."

Vexed and somewhat astonished by this reaction, Beecher turned his boundless energy toward a more dramatic demonstration of his showmanship; he would "auction off" a slave. In late May 1856, he arranged to have a small mulatto woman brought from a plantation near Staunton, Virginia, and he "sold" her to his congregation in a mock auction. While many questioned the authenticity of the arrangements, there remained little doubt of its impact on Beecher's flock. After his sermon and the final hymn of the morning, Beecher called the twenty-two-year-old slave, Sarah, to his pulpit. Sarah walked forward slowly, head bowed, and took a seat near the famous preacher. She lifted her eyes, stared at the spellbound audience, and burst into sobs. Her plight tugged at the heart of the most stolid Congregationalist as Beecher's inflamed rhetoric described her life. Daughter of a well-known white citizen, she had been put up for sale by her own father. The slave dealer involved contacted Beecher through a mutual friend and they struck a deal allowing Sarah to go north with the promise of either her return or the full manumission fee.

Beecher's description of her plight and his demand for "bids" for the young woman unleashed a frenzy of generosity amid tears, sobs and shrieks. Twenty-dollar notes were stuffed into the collection boxes and many tore off bracelets, necklaces and watches and pressed them on the beleaguered ushers. For half an hour contributions poured in, $833 in all, more than was needed to buy Sarah's freedom.

Four years later, on February 5, 1860, Beecher's congregation also bought freedom for Sally Maria Diggs. Known as "Pink," her one sixteenth African blood qualified her for a life of slavery in the South. The youngster, about nine, as white as any of the children of Beecher's church members, was born into slavery in Port Tobacco, Maryland. She saw all of her family sold deeper into the South with the exception of her grandmother, with whom she lived. Her owner, however, decided to sever even this arrangement and sell her for $900. Her predicament came to the attention of a young Episcopal seminarian, John Falkner Blake, of Alexandria, Virginia, and he contacted Beecher. Blake gave a bond guaranteeing either the $900 or Pink's return, and she traveled to Brooklyn. In another emotional outburst, Beecher's flock contributed as much toward Pink's manumission as they had for Sarah's. Later Pink changed her name to Rose Ward Diggs in honor of Rose Terry, a local poet who contributed a valuable ring, and Henry Ward Beecher, who had made her freedom possible.

Blake received the money and went through the legalities necessary to free Pink. He first had to purchase her himself and then officially manumit her. Here is the text of the papers he filed.

Whereas on the fifth day of February in the year of our Lord eighteen hundred and sixty the Reverend Henry Ward Beecher of the city of Brooklyn state of New York presented to the congregation of said city of which congregation he is the pastor the case of Sally Maria Diggs, usually called Pink who was then a slave child offered for sale in the city of Washington District of Columbia and whereas the said Beecher and congregation were desirous that the said slave child should be set free in order that she might not be separated from her grandmother with whom she had lived up to that date and Whereas a contribution of money was made by the said congregation on the date above mentioned for the purpose of securing the freedom of the said slave child which money was put into my hand by the said Beecher with instructions to take the proper steps for securing the freedom of the said slave child and Whereas on the eighth day of February in the year of our Lord eighteen hundred and sixty in pursuance of said instructions I did purchase the said slave from the owner John C. Cook of the city of Washington D.C. for the sum of nine hundred dollars and received from the said Cook a bill of sale of the said slave to myself and Whereas the said slave child is now my legal property

Now be it known that I John Falkner Blake now residing in the city of Alexandria in the State of Virginia for divers and good causes and considerations me thereto moving have relieved (sic) from slavery liberated manumitted and set free and by these presents to hereby release from slavery manumit and set free my mulatto girl named Sally Maria Diggs commonly called "Pink" aged about nine years and able to work and gain a sufficient livelihood and maintenance and her the said Mulatto girl named Sally Maria Diggs I do declare to be henceforth free manumitted and forever discharged from all manner of servitude or service to me- my executors administrators heirs and assigns forever. In testimony whereof I have here to set my hand and seal this eleventh day of February one thousand eight hundred and sixty.

*   *   *   *   *   *

City and County of Washington

District of Columbia

On this eleventh day of February one thousand eight hundred and sixty before me a justice of the peace is and for said city county and district came personally the above named John Falkner Blake and being known to me as the person who executed the above deed of manumission and duly acknowledged the instrument of manumission to be his act and deed for the purpose therein mentioned.

Thomas Donn (seal)

Justice of the Peace

*   *   *   *   *   *

On May 27, 1927, during the Plymouth Church's eightieth year, a postscript to that dramatic event took place that rivaled in excitement anything that Henry Ward Beecher ever conjured up.

During a special Sunday evening service, an elderly, light skinned black woman walked slowly to the pulpit to be introduced to a cheering audience. The wife of a prominent Washington, D.C. attorney named James Hunt, she had been, sixty-seven years earlier, Sally Maria Diggs. Pink, the former slave, had returned to Brooklyn to honor the memory of her benefactor.

During the first few years of the conflict Henry Ward Beecher raised money for equipping local regiments and spoke endlessly on patriotic themes. Before a group of Sons of Connecticut at the Fifth Avenue Hotel in October 1861, he said:

"I have never had the faintest doubt as to the result of this contest. Slavery will go to hell whence it came from not that we are richer, stronger and better than the South, but because God is fighting against it. We shall conquer the rebels not in our own strength but the Almighty will lay them across our knees and we will spank them in the natural order of Providence."

Beecher's constant patriotic work wore him down and in the fall of 1863 he decided to take a "rest" trip to England. He didn't get much rest.

Shut off from its main supply of cotton, Great Britain had suffered severe unemployment in its textile industry. This had created great hostility to President Lincoln's government in some parts of England, and Beecher decided to make several speeches to strengthen the federal cause and counteract southern propaganda. He spoke to chilly receptions in Liverpool and Manchester, hotbeds of Confederate sympathy. Although

Beecher may not have swayed all of his listeners, he did impress them. One newspaper reported that "Mr. Beecher's audacity in lecturing at all had a trace of sublimity in it." Hostile audiences held anti-Beecher placards, quoting him as saying in 1861, during the Trent Affair -- in which a Union warship had seized two Confederate diplomats being carried on a British ship -- that "the best blood of England must flow for the outrage England had perpetrated on America," and they jeered and heckled him. He wrote to his friend Theodore Tilton, however, that he felt some sort of "out-of-body sensation" while delivering his talks, never fearing the threats he heard or read about."I have a perverse and ludicrous sympathy with the rascals," he confessed, "If I could only establish a duality and keep one self speaking I think with the other I would go down into the crowd and tell them how to point their mischief a good deal more wittily and efficiently." And he wrote to his brother Charles, "In spite of their faults I like the English. Put that in your pipe and smoke it."

Beecher returned home feeling that he had helped America's beleaguered friends in England by supporting their anti-slavery convictions. He had used his skills to defend his country and its goals. Feted at the Brooklyn Academy of Music and at his church, he continued to speak out for President Lincoln's policies, campaigned for Lincoln's re-election in 1864, and became the president's choice as the main speaker for the flag-restoring ceremonies at Fort Sumter, South Carolina, after the fort was recovered by Union forces in 1865.

Abraham Lincoln once remarked to Henry M. Field, a New York editor, that no person in modern or even ancient times had "so productive a mind" as Henry Ward Beecher.

In post-war years Beecher campaigned for women's rights, temperance, and Jewish-Christian relationships. After a highly publicized adultery trial in 1875, he lost some of his glitter, even though he was exonerated. He died on March 3, 1887, at 124 Hicks Street, and was buried in Green-Wood Cemetery, in Brooklyn.

Canonical Inflation

I received a letter last week from a recent, well-known, retiree, who wondered why the Canon had not kept pace with inflation. I wrote back to Alan Greenspan (Head of the Federal Reserve) that I would try my hand at correcting things.

Is it any wonder that so many people are still fascinated by the goings on at <u>222B</u> Baker Street? After climbing the famous <u>eighteen</u> steps we meet the world's only consulting detective, Sherlock Holmes, the expert <u>double</u> stick player with an addiction to an <u>eight</u> percent solution of cocaine. He is generally joined in adventure by his friend, Dr. John H. Watson, veteran of the <u>Third</u> Afghan War, and Holmes' brother, Mycroft, <u>eight years</u> older, and many pounds heavier.

In the street below there is a dense fog, and we can barely see people getting into <u>five-wheelers</u>. We meet arch villains, like Professor Moriarty, so evil, despite his brilliance in authoring the <u>Trinomial</u> Theorem, which had a European vogue.

We simply can't resist following Holmes and Watson through some their most fascinating cases: <u>The Duo Cyclist</u>, <u>The Six Orange Pips</u>, <u>The Seven Napoleons,</u> <u>The Four Gables</u>, and <u>The Third Stain</u>. In today's case, the Dying Detective, we hear of the deadly Asian disease the <u>Black Fivemosa Corruption</u>. And we are always somewhere different, whether on the moor with John Straker trying to cut Silver Blaze's <u>fiveleg,</u> or on the high seas on the Gloria Scott's <u>fivecastle</u>.

In The Sign of Five, Mary Morstan sees Holmes at the behest of her employer, Mrs. Cecil Fiveester. Mary is sent pearls in a mysterious fashion and then receives a letter directing her to be at the fourth pillar from the left outside the Lyceum Theater at eight o'clock. If she is distrustful to bring three friends. It appears that Mary will soon inherit a fivetune and poor Watson will never win her. When Watson hears of this he strikes his fivehead in despair. In fact there are a lot of fiveheads mentioned in the Canon. Vincent Spaulding has a splash of acid on his fivehead; Count Von Kramm had a high white fivehead, and after a fight in the Duo Cyclist, Holmes had a discoloured lump upon his fivehead. There are more but these four examples will do.

In MUSG, Holmes says that the advent of Charles the Second was already fiveseen. In the Four Students, there is cheating involved with the Fivetescu Scholarship. In The Missing Four Quarter Holmes searches for Stauntons in his commonplace book. Here he finds Arthur H. Staunton, the rising young fiveger. And, lastly, since Holmes quoted thrice from his favorite Shakespearean play, Thirteenth Night, we should now celebrate his birthday on January 7th.

I must end this now with apologies to Victor Borge, who came up with this inflationary scheme.

The Canonical Balance of Trade

Some time ago, at a meeting of the Epilogues, in Chatham, N.J., a discussion arose as to how many villains and/or murderers were domestic and how many were imported. The domestic criminals are too numerous to mention but the imports we can handle. Some committed crimes outside of England, in places like Pennsylvania's Vermissa Valley, Utah, Hungary, and India. Some of the émigrés became criminals through no fault of their own; some sought vengeance and got it; others committed no indictable crime. But their actions all fall into the category of either villain, murderer, bigamist, spy, suicide, despot, or blackmailer. One murderer came from central Africa, one from the deep blue sea, and one ... well, we don't know exactly what it did but we know where it came from, and it was baleful, to say the least.

Most of our imported malefactors are individuals but we do have three groups. Some are human (very human in the case of our bigamist), some are not, and as you might guess, most of them come from America - nine individuals and three groups. In second place, having four, are Germany (although that is not always clear), and Italy. Australia and India share third place honors with three each. France and South Africa have two, and the rest are from the Andaman Islands, Austria, Brazil, Greece, Russia, and Central America, a veritable United Nations of dysfunction.

Beginning with the U. S. of A., we have three groups of murderers. One specialized in extortion, one in polygamy, and the third in sailing. I refer, of course, to the Scowrers, the Mormons, and Captain James Calhoun and his mates on the Lone Star. Individual Yankee murderers include John Douglas, alias John McMurdo, a.k.a. Birdy Edwards (really an Irishman; self defense), Jefferson Hope (vengeance), Abe Slaney (self defense), James Winter, alias Morecroft, John Garrideb and Killer Evans. Ted Baldwin (probably already a murderer) attempted to kill John Douglas; Joseph Stangerson and Enoch Drebber, polygamists, drove Lucie Ferrier to her grave; Hatty Doran became a bigamist unknowingly, and J. Neil Gibson is just a plain, old, nasty s.o.b.

The Germans include spies Adolph Meyer, Hugo Oberstein and Von Bork, and the murderers are Oberstein and Lysander (Fritz) Stark, the likely killer of Jeremiah Hayling, the hydraulic engineer. The Italian murderers are Beppo and Gennaro Lucca (self defense). Black Gorgiano, the Red Circle don, is a villain, most probably a murderer, and Pietro Venucci is a cut-throat.

The three allegedly Sikh signees, Mahomet Singh, Dost Akbar and Abdullah Khan, committed their murder in India.

The Aussies are Henry (Holy) Peters, guilty of theft and attempted murder; Charles McCarthy, the blackmailer, and John Turner, who has already murdered Down Under, and who does it again, this time doing in McCarthy. France pitches in with the Fournayes, Henri and Madame, the former a spy (as Eduardo Lucas) and the latter his murderer. South Africa supplies us with two villains, one who turns out to be very protective, and the other who forces a maiden to marry him without a proper license. Bob Carruthers, the decent crook, tries to murder Roaring Jack Woodley, but is unsuccessful and only wounds him.

From the sunny Andaman Islands we have Tonga, who murdered Bartholomew Sholto, and Greece offers Sophie Kratides, who, we infer, knocked off her brother's murderers in Buda- Pesth. From Brazil comes the scheming Maria Pinto who, with her hot tropical blood, commits suicide and tries to blame Grace Dunbar for murdering her. Austria provides us with one of the worst of our killers, the purring Baron Gruner, while Russia gives us Anna Coram who kills Willoughby Smith quite by accident. If only her HMO (Health Maintenance Organization) had allowed her another pair of pince-nez. From Central America we chip in with Don Murillo, el Tigro, who has murdered Miss Burnett's hubby back home. Imported all the way from Ubanghi is Radix Pedis Diaboli, the silent killer, who also drives people nuts. The Atlantic Ocean has provided us with cyanea capillata who whips people to death, and last, but definitely far from least, that Giant Rat, Sumatra's pride and joy. We don't know what it did but it must have been something quite awful since the world is still not yet prepared to hear about it.

Coats and Cloaks

A frock coat is defined by Jack Tracy as "a body-coat, usually double-breasted and with a full skirt, worn by men." And more characters wore frock coats than any other kind. Oddly enough, accompanying this description in <u>The Ultimate Sherlock Holmes Encyclopedia</u>, there is a Sidney Paget sketch of Lysander Stark (ENGR) wearing a frock coat, although the Canon offers no description of this. Among our frock coat aficionados are: Grimesby Roylott (SPEC), Professor Presbury (CREE), Enoch Drebber of Salt Lake City (heavy broadcloth, STUD), Colonel Ross (SILV) and Holmes (NORW, HOUN and EMPT). In EMPT, in disguise as the gnarled old book seller, his frock coat is seedy. A much neater frock coat, obviously, is worn by Sir James Damery (dark, ILLU).

Many wear black frock coats: Alexander Holder (BERY), Lawler (VALL), Hosmer Angel (IDEN), Henry Baker (BLUE, rusty), Percy Trevelyan (RESI), Lord Robert St. Simon (NOBL) and Jabez Wilson (REDH). Wilson apparently never cleans his. Neither, it seems, does Dr. Mortimer (HOUN). Wilson's is not over-clean and the good Dr.'s, although not black, is dingy. Yucch. Mr. Merryweather (REDH), by contrast, has one that is oppressively respectable. What a difference. Old Ralph and Mr. Kent (BLAN) wore black, too, but they owned plain coats, not frock coats. There were also great coats, worn by Watson and Holmes when they broke into Charles Augustus Milverton's home (CHAS); and by Tobias Gregson in (REDC). Overcoats were worn by Holmes and Watson in CREE; by Holmes in STUD, and by Watson in BRUC. Jabez Wilson, in addition to his frock coat, wore a faded brown overcoat with a wrinkled velvet collar. It must have been very cold the day he visited Baker Street. Pea jackets were worn by Lestrade (NOBL) when he trawled The Serpentine; by John McMurdo (VALL), and by Holmes (SIGN and REDH). Anticipating a frigid vigil near the moat at Birlstone Manor House, Holmes warns Inspector MacDonald and White Mason to wear their warmest coats (VALL). Holmes and Watson followed this same advice and wore heavy coats in (ABBE). Poor Charles McCarthy (BOSC). He had hardly a coat to his back when he returned to England.

Ulsters, those long, loose overcoats, were worn by Holmes in STUD, by both Holmes and Watson in BLUE, and by Hatty Doran in NOBL. Holmes wore a shiny, seedy coat while undercover in BERY, and while Hugh Boone had on a tattered coat, Neville St. Clair started the day wearing a dark coat (TWIS). Heading out to do his dirty deed, John Straker wore a large Mackintosh overcoat (SILV), while poor, duped, John McFarland had on a light summer overcoat (NORW). Lestrade (BOSC) wore a light brown dust coat and Anthony (HOUN) was rusty-coated. Jefferson Hope wore a long brown overcoat in (STUD).

The cloak wearers were few and far between but they are well known to us. They Include: Holmes (BOSC) in a long grey traveling cloak; Mary Morstan (SIGN) who was muffled in a dark cloak; John Turner (BOSC) in a grey cloak that he dropped, and Mycroft, in a heavy black cloak tipped at the collar with red, when he drove the brougham in (FINA). And when it poured, both Stanley Hopkins (GOLD) and John Openshaw (FIVE) wore shining waterproofs.

Astrakhan is lustrous, closely curled wool, coming from Astrakhan, near the Caspian Sea. Three Canonical coats are in this category, and they belong to the worst man in London, to a king who is six-and-a-half feet tall, and to a famous valetudinarian. The odious Charles Augustus Milverton (CHAS) wore an Astrakhan, shaggy overcoat; the King of Bohemia's coat had heavy bands of Astrakhan slashed across the sleeves and fronts of his double breasted coat (SCAN), and poor nervous Thaddeus Sholto (SIGN) had a long, befrogged top-coat with astrakhan collar and cuff. Even with his huge coat and his rabbit-skin cap with the hanging lappets which covered his ears, I'll bet he was still shivering.

Hold on to your Hats

When it came to hats, Arthur Conan Doyle was no Lily Dache. He did, however, love certain headgear, especially the cap, which was his favorite. He described sixteen different kinds of caps ranging from plain (Patrick Cairns, BLAC), to rabbit skin with hanging lappets (Thaddeus Sholto, SIGN). In between those two we find: close-fitting (Holmes, BOSC), ear-flapped traveling (Holmes, SILV), small velvet smoking Culverton Smith, (DYIN), flat black velvet (Boss McGinty, VALL), thick, black, (John McMurdo, VALL), mob (Susan Dobney, LADY), cloth (Holmes, HOUN), old (Selden, HOUN), trim (Susan Cushing, CARD), country (Martha, LAST), and greasy leather (Hugh Boone, TWIS), yucch.

All of the above are mentioned only once. Three Canonical characters wear peaked caps (Inspector Bradstreet, TWIS); Captain Marvin of the Coal and Iron Police, (VALL); and Lord Saltire, his in blue with a white chevron on the peak, (PRIO), three sport cloth caps (Bob Carruthers, SOLI, Fitzroy Simpson, SILV, John Hopley Neligan, BLAC), and two wear soft caps (Victor Hatherley, ENGR); and Ted Baldwin, as Hargrave, (VALL).

Then there are the undescribed caps worn by the jockeys in the Wessex Cup. They are red, pink, yellow, black and purple (SILV).

And that is the cap department.

The next biggest category is top hats. Grimesby Roylott's is black (SPEC), Jabez Wilson's is frayed (REDH), Lord Mt. James's is very broad-brimmed (MISS) James Windbank's is shiny (IDEN), Hall Pycroft's is very shiny (STOC), Sir James Damery's is lucent (ILLU), Enoch Drebber's is a plain top hat (STUD), as is the old Shikari, Colonel Sebastian Moran's. He wore an opera hat, similar to a top hat (EMPT).

Three characters, all from SIGN, wore turbans. Mary Morstan's was small and of the same dull hue as her outfit, a sombre grayish beige, and both Achmet and Thaddeus Sholto's Khitmutgar wore the yellow variety.

There are six references to bonnets. Irene Adler was the daintiest thing under one (SCAN); Henry Baker's was Scotch (BLUE); Hattie Doran (NOBL), Effie Munro (YELL), and Mrs. Saunders (3GAR) all wore them, and Holmes had a wee bit of a bee in his, according to Alec McDonald (VALL).

Alexander Holder had a shiny hat (BERY), Mr. Merryweather's hat was very shiny (REDH), while two unlikely looking murderers wore straw hats (Jack Stapleton, (HOUN); Josiah Amberley, (RETI). Sherlock Holmes wore a broad, black hat as the non-denominational clergyman in SCAN and a priest's hat in FINA.

Colonel Valentine Walters got his broad-brimmed hat knocked off in BRUC, Count Von Kramm's hat was broad-brimmed (SCAN), and Robert St. Simon wore a curly brimmed hat in

NOBL. The bowler people are Mr. Kent (BLAN), and Henry Baker, owner of the battered billycock, the very seedy and disreputable hard felt hat he lost in his scuffle with the toughs in BLUE. We have three felt wearers: Grant Munro with his brown wide-awake, which is soft felt (YELL), and two men from VALL: Lawler, also soft felt, and Ted Baldwin who wore felt, but broad-brimmed and black.

That most dangerous crook in Chicago, Abe Slaney, wore a Panama hat (DANC) and that wild, profane, and godless man, Hugo Baskerville, had a plumed hat in his portrait (HOUN).

It wasn't easy to pick a winner among the wearers of all of these fancy chapeaus, but one does stand out in a pejorative way. Watson said she wore a large curling feather in her broad brimmed hat which was tilted in a coquettish Duchess of Devonshire fashion over her ear. He thought it was a slate colored, broad-brimmed straw hat, with a feather of brickish red. And when Mary Sutherland (IDEN) left he referred to her vacuous face and her preposterous hat.

Anatole of Paris would have loved her.

If Sherlock Holmes Could Do It Why Couldn't Others?

In EMPT, Holmes explains his return to life after his alleged descent into the waters of Reichenbach Falls. "It came about in this way. The instant that the Professor had disappeared, it struck me what a real extraordinarily lucky chance Fate had placed in my way. I knew that Moriarty was not the only man who had sworn my death. There were at least three others whose desire for vengeance upon me would only be increased by the death of their leader. They were all most dangerous men. One or the other would certainly get me. On the other hand, if all the world was convinced that I was dead they would take liberties, these men, they would soon lay themselves open, and sooner or later I could destroy them. Then it would be time for me to announce that I was still in the land of the living. So rapidly does the brain act that I believe I had thought this all out before Professor Moriarty had reached the bottom of the Reichenbach Falls."

And of course Holmes did just as he said.

And if Holmes could do this why couldn't others?

John Douglas had been John McMurdo who had been Birdy Edwards. He had escaped death in the Vermissa Valley, in California, and in Birlstone. He had been murdered by one of Professor Moriarty's numerous accomplices on board the Palmyra, probably pushed overboard in a gale.

How do we know this? Because Ivy Douglas told us so. But why should we believe her? Would it not make sense to take another identity in South Africa? Perhaps a Jack McDonald would appear in the Transvaal to take up gold mining once more. Edwards had as many reasons to disappear as Sherlock Holmes. He had the Scowrers after him and they were certainly a murderous bunch. Edwards's taking on yet another identity makes sense and until we know that his body was recovered and that he really had lost his life.

There was another charmer who was supposedly sent on a year at sea to rid him of his fratricidal tendencies. Sadly enough, the log of the liner Bohemia indicated that three children on board died in agony, their limbs stretched out abnormally, in what seemed to be curare poisoning. Did little Jackie Ferguson straighten out at all?

Three nautical miles off Southampton the Lone Star met up with the Shenandoah, a former Confederate naval raider. All members of the Lone Star's crew first scuttled their ship and then transferred to the giant vessel for a long, long voyage to Melbourne.

It's possible, no?

The Curious Case of a Curious Man Named Wilson

One would think, considering contemporary statistics, that the most common surname among Canonical references would be Smith. Or Johnson. Or Williams. But it doesn't seem to work that way. Now, I mean an individual surname, only one to a family. In short, you can't count the eight Baskervilles (HOUN), or the six Falders (SHOS), or the four Garridebs (3GAR) but there are only seven different Smiths (Culverton, DYIN; Violet, SOLI; Joseph, the Mormon Leader, STUD; Mordecai, the boatman, SIGN; Willoughby, the secretary, GOLD; Smith and Wesson, the gun manufacturer, VALL; and the Smith Mortimer succession case, GOLD); only four Johnsons (an Oxford rugby player, MISS; Shinwell, ILLU; Sidney, BRUC; Theophilus, HOUN); and only four Williams (Mawson and Williams, BLAC; the prizefighter, SIGN; Charlie, a Scowrers' victim, VALL; James Baker, a neighbor of Aloysius Garcia, WIST). None of these surnames come close to being the most popular in the Canon. One surprise contender is Mason, and there are five of them (the platelayer, BRUC; the man who escaped justice because of a lack of a reliable blood test, STUD; John, the trainer, SHOS; Mrs. the nurse, SUSS; and detective White, VALL).

In the four category we find Anderson, Hudson, Morton, Brown, and Ferguson. The Andersons include the soldier killed in the Boer War (BLAN); the Fulworth constable, (LION); the Anderson murders in N.C. (HOUN), and <u>Sophy</u>, the barque

(FIVE). The Hudsons are: a Klu Kluxer, (FIVE); the evil sailor, (GLOR); Morse of Kennington Road, (SIXN); and Mrs. of 221B.

The Mortons are represented by the inspector from Scotland Yard (DYIN); an Oxford Rugby player (MISS); Cyril, fiancé of Violet Smith (SOLI); and Morton and Waylight (REDC).

Among the Browns are: Josiah (SIXN); Scotland Yard Sam; Lt. Bromley (SIGN); and the bully, Silas (SILV). Here are the Fergusons: Dr. Becher (ENGR); J.Neil Gibson's secretary (THOR); the retired sea captain (3GAB); and the London tea broker (SUSS).

The winner, as you may have guessed, is Wilson. There are no less than ten of them, and oddly enough, even four different Wilsons in one case (VALL).

Here we go. There's the notorious canary trainer (BLAC); the partner of Jack Prendergast (GLOR); one of the constables at Yoxley Old Place (GOLD); the manager of a district messenger office (HOUN); red-headed pawnbroker Jabez (REDH); and General Sir Archdale of the Bengal Artillery (SIGN). The quartet from VALL are the sergeant in the Sussex Constabulary; Bartholomew, the district ruler of the Ancient Order of Freemen in Chicago; a Scowrer; and Steve, the alleged nom de guerre of Birdie Edwards.

Four separate Wilsons in one case.

Why Wilson? Your Canonical guess is as good as mine.

B for Beautiful

In Watson's Eyes

Nancy Barclay (CROO): She was a woman of great beauty, and that even now, when she has been married for upward of thirty years, she is still of a striking and queenly appearance. Lady Brackenstall (ABBE): Seldom have I seen so graceful a figure, so womanly a presence, and so beautiful a face. Lady Francis Carfax (LADY): A beautiful woman, still in fresh middle age Alice Charpentier (STUD): an uncommonly fine girl. Hatty Doran (NOBL): A very lovely woman. Ivy Douglas (VALL): She was a beautiful woman, tall, dark and slender, some twenty years younger than her husband. Maria Pinto (THOR): was very beautiful, rare and wonderful in her beauty. Grace Dunbar (THOR): A very beautiful woman.

Lucy Ferrier (STUD): as fair a specimen of American girlhood as could be found in the whole Pacific slope; the flower of Utah. Beryl Garcia Stapleton (HOUN); I had heard someone describe her as being a beauty. A brunette, slim, elegant and tall, a proud, finely cut face, sensitive mouth and beautiful dark, eager eyes. Violet De Merville (ILLU): She is beautiful but with the ethereal other-world beauty of some fanatic whose thoughts are set on high.

Lady Trelawney Hope (SECO): I had often heard of the beauty of the youngest daughter of the Duke of Belminster…subtle, delicate charm and the beautiful coloring of that exquisite head.

Isadora Klein (3GAB): tall, queenly, a perfect figure, with two wonderful Spanish eyes that looks murder at us both. Emilia Lucca (REDC): a tall and beautiful woman. Ettie Shafter (VALL): a very beautiful woman. Mrs. Godfrey Staunton (MISS): young and beautiful. Mary Morstan (SIGN): Her face had neither regularity of feature nor beauty of complexion, but her expression was sweet and amiable. Alice Morphy (CREE): a very perfect girl both in mind and body. Miss Morrison (CROO): striking looking. Alice Turner (BOSC): one of the most lovely young women that I have ever seen in my life. Brenda Tregannis (DEVI): A very beautiful girl Violet Smith (SOLI) young and beautiful.

I guess that beauty is in the eye of the beholder and John H. Watson had that kind of an eye.

I Don't Feel So Well

Canonical Sickness and Disabilities

It makes sense that there are a host of ailing, crippled and very high strung characters in the Canon. After all, the man who described them had suffered endlessly while taking the Queen's shilling. He had been struck in the shoulder by a Jezail bullet, contracted enteric fever, and was invalided out of the service, his health irretrievably ruined. He couldn't stand noise or excitement, was weak and emaciated, held his injured left arm in a stiff and unnatural manner, had a haggard face, was thin as a lath, and limped impatiently. All this from having undergone hardship and sickness. And so it seems proper that he would create so many fellow sufferers.

Physical ailments are found throughout the Canon, ranging from clubfoot to aortic aneurisms, to a particularly virulent kind of consumption. But emotional problems are present, too, as characters succumb to alcoholism, cocaine and opium addictions, brain fevers and broken hearts.

Drunkeness does in more characters than any other weakness. It that category we have the evil sailors Hudson and Peter Carey, Enoch Drebber, Elias Openshaw, Eustace Brackenstall, Mr. Norlett, Murphy, the gipsy horse dealer on the moor, Jim Browner, the fictitious Tom Dennis, Watson's unhappy brother,

Toller, and Mrs. Tangey. Several of the aforementioned imbibers may still be imbibing but four of them die ghastly deaths, and Hudson, who never got his 'pology, simply disappears under mysterious circumstances.

Weak hearts have their place. Here we have Fitzroy McPherson (from rheumatic fever), Captain Morstan, Trevor, Sr., and Lady Beatrice Falder, who also suffers from dropsy.

And consumption (cough, cough). It strikes down Mrs. Godfrey Staunton, Fraser (who is instrumental in Baskerville/Vanderleur/Stapleton setting up a school), and the allegedly dying English lady at the Englischer Hof.

Lameness comes next. There are six amputees mentioned in the leg department: Jonathan Small, Francis Prosper, Josiah Amberley, the harmless tradesman who gets shot at by Major Sholto, the newspaper vendor in ILLU and the Confederate General John B. Hood. Watson limps around periodically with a damaged tendo Achillis and, as Holmes predicts, so does John Turner, with his right leg.

The elderly, 5-foot-tall, deformed man, in EMPT turns out to be Holmes in one of his better disguises, but Henry Wood really was crippled from his imprisonment in India. Culverton Smith was twisted in the shoulders and back like one who has suffered from rickets in childhood and although Hugh Boone appears a cripple, with a twisted lip, he is just malingering for his two pounds per diem. Holmes also specializes in this useful art as he proves in DYIN and REIG and in SIGN, when he exhibits the proper workhouse cough. And the Russian "nobleman" does a good job on catalepsy, fooling Dr. Percy Trevelyan. Holmes, unimpressed, claims he has used this ruse on occasion, too.

Some of the suffering is of an emotional nature. Witness nervous wrecks like Alexander Holder, John Hector McFarlane, the valetudinarian Thaddeus Sholto, the unhappy merchant Achmet, Harry Pinner, Mrs. Bernstone, Thorneycroft Huxtable and Helen Stoner. Old Abrahams is in mortal terror of his life; Blessington is in a pitiable state of prostration, and the rest are merely shivering in their shoes. They should have listened to Oscar Hammerstein and whistled a happy tune.

Brain fever has also struck down Rachell Howells, Percy Phelps, Sarah Cushing, Alice Rucastle and Nancy Barclay, all suffering from what today we would call a nervous breakdown. Even Holmes, after working at times up to five days at a stretch without rest, crashes and descends into a black depression. We also have General DeMerville, a broken man, and broken-hearted Lucy Ferrier and Sir James Walter, both of whom pine away from the indignities heaped upon them.

Douglas Maberley dies from pneumonia, and an aortic aneurism takes care of Jefferson Hope, who just may have met his maker with a satisfied smile on his face. Apoplexy lies low Colonel Barclay and Trevor, Sr. Different strokes for different folks. Among the more exotic ailments are Major Sholto's enlarged spleen, Jack Ferguson's weak spine, Ricoletti's club foot, Professor Presbury's creepy-deepies, Lord Mount-James's gout, Trevor's sister's diphtheria, John Turner's diabetes, Sir Charles Baskerville's dyspnoea, John Hebron's and Roger Baskerville's yellow fever, Lady Maynooth's cataracts, Mr. Farquhar's St. Vitus's Dance (maybe Wilson Kemp had that, too, since he was jerking around so much), Shinwell Johnson's scurvy, Von Herder's blindness, Hosmer Angel's quinsy and swollen glands, Jonathan Small's ague, Geoffrey Emsworth's ichthyosis, Ettie Shafter's typhoid fever, Colonel Warburton's and Isadora Persano's madness and Professor Coram's je ne sais quoi. Even more exotic are two weirdo diseases that are mentioned but never caught by anyone we know: tapanuli fever and black Formosan corruption.

We seemed to have omitted the deaf and the myopic. Included in the hard-of-hearing are William Kirwin's mother, the Widow MacNamara, and our favorite butler, Barrymore. In the weak eyes department we have Mary Sutherland, Hosmer Angel and Anna of the golden pince-nez.

Among our addicts, or part-time addicts, we have Holmes needling cocaine, Isa Whitney smoking opium and both Sir Jabez Gilchrist and Arthur Holder gambling. And there is another addiction, one that affected Holmes and John Douglas, that of tobacco. They both suffered from the lack of it in DYIN and VALL, respectively.

And we even have one very vague ailment. Dr. Shlesinger was recovering from a disease contracted in the exercise of his apostolic duties.

Amen.

Take two aspirin and call me in the morning.

Present Laughter (Or LOL)

We don't find much hilarity in the Canon and I can think of very few occasions when comical moments appear. Toby, our favorite spaniel/lurcher, provides one when his sense of smell takes him to a barrel of creosote (SIGN), and Holmes certainly plays the clown when he pulls Henry Baker's hat down on his head so that only his nose shows (BLUE). A finger-down-the-page search in the 60 cases comes up with 124 Laughs in the Canon in 52 cases; 8 are barren of frivolity (ABBE, BERYL, CREE, LADY, REDC, THOR, 3STU, VEIL). Some of the minor laughs include Inspector Bradstreet's "He He" (TWIS) and Arthur/Harry Pinner's "Ha Ha," showing a tooth stuffed with gold (STOC). Holmes also offers a "Ha Ha" in STUD as does Mr. Frankland (HOUN).

Holmes laughed a lot, 36 times, in fact, in a variety of cases, sometimes noiselessly (BLUE), heartily (SOLI), good-humoredly (GLOR), and good naturedly (PRIO). But there was more than laughter. Five characters chuckled: the perspicacious Inspector Baynes (WIST), the obnoxious Charles Augustus Milverton (CHAS), the villainous Baron Gruner (ILLU), White Mason (VALL) and even the German, Von Herling (LAST). And Holmes is the biggest chuckler of all, 20 times on different occasions, so that plus his 36 laughs is a total 56 yuks out of 124, some 44%. Not bad for a guy who is not exactly the life of the party.

Violet Smith blushes when she laughs; Jack Woodley offers a brutal, exultant, laugh; and Bob Carruthers' laugh is a bitter one, all in SOLI. Abe Slaney also offers a bitter laugh (DANC); Rachel Howells shrieks laughter (MUSG); Lestrade laughs loudly and Jonas Oldacre provides an uneasy laugh in Norw. There are a host of other characters who laugh: Isadora Klein, Henry Baker (shamefaced and hearty), Sarah Cushing (mockingly), Charles Augustus Milverton (he laughs with fear vibrating in his voice, just before he meets his maker), Violet Hunter, who can't help laughing at Jephro Rucastle's stories, Victor Hatherly, James Windibank, Colonel James Damery, Von Bork, Harold Stackhurst, Joseph Harrison, Reuben Hayes (a false laugh), Jabez Wilson (heavily), Professor Coram, Thaddeus Sholto, Jack Stapleton, Beryl Stapleton, Sir Henry Baskerville, Lucy Ferrier, Alec Cunningham, Percy Trevalian, and the hired hands in Serpentine Avenue in SCAN.

Some laughter is not quite funny as it comes from the lepers in BLAN, and the Tregennis brothers as they are carted off to the asylum (DEVI), and to Mrs. Hudson who is hysterical when she sees Sherlock Holmes after his great hiatus (EMPT). Add to these Watson's laughs (SHOS, YELL, FIVE, GREE, REDH, SCAN, SIGN, HOUN), and we have a lot of guffaws. Some peculiar laughing goes on in one of the nastier cases. In GREE, Holmes and Watson both laugh but the twitchy Wilson Kemp giggles on no less than 5 occasions, bringing the laughter meter there up to seven.

The winner in the laugh department is VALL as we have laughs from Holmes, Ivy Douglas, Mike Scanlan, Tiger Cormac, Jack

Douglas, Jack McMurdo (4) and Boss McGinty (4) for a total of 13. It seems that it was not only The Valley of Fear but also The Valley of Laughs.

For our older Sherlockians, I might say, T'aint funny McGee.

A Letter from Professor Presbury

Now who, outside of the Canon, would the formidable Professor write to? Through diligent searching in that tin box belonging to Dr. Watson, the archives of Trevor Bennett, and especially information gleaned from a greatly embarrassed Edith, the professor's daughter, I discovered a poignant letter sent to an American politician, or rather, to a retired American politician, to ascertain what could be done about an intimate problem that said politician was not too embarrassed to discuss on nation-wide TV.

This is the letter.

Dear Robert Dole (Dole, once a presidential candidate, had been huckstering for Viagra on television).

This is not easy to say and it is difficult to put into words, but I have been told by people I trust that you have a solution to my problems, where a single blue pill would do for me more than all of my ivy climbing and creeping around scaring the bejeepers out of my assistant and my own daughter and having my neck all chewed up by Roy.

I must admit that I have had a bit of fun playing Tarzan but I would rather get down on to solid ground again as Mr. Sherlock Holmes has noticed my horny knuckles and has surmised that not only my knuckles but the rest of me is rather horny, too. Please advise if the cost of your miracle blue pills are really 20 pounds a pop and whether I can get them for a reduced price from Her Royal Majesty's Veterans Administration. I am too old to continue visiting Prague for the latest information on this monkey business

Salaciously yours,

Professor Presbury

Smoke Gets in your Eyes

Although Professor Coram (GOLD) smoked more than anyone else in the Canon (1,000 cigarettes a fortnight from Ionides of Alexandria - some 3 1/2 packs a day), someone is smoking in most cases, but not all. Not by a long shot. Sometimes these habits are not definitely spelled out but rather implied. We may infer from the mention of cigars, pipes, or tobacco in (CARD, MAZA, YELL, REDC, 3STU, and MUSG), that someone will smoke these items, or has smoked them, but no one is actually smoking them. Holmes says to Mrs. Warren, "You don't object to tobacco, I take it? Thank you. Watson, the matches," and the disjecta membra from Emilia Lucca's room contains two burned "match" and a cigarette end (REDC). Holmes deduces Grant Munro's strength by the way he has bitten the stem of his nice old brier pipe, and his wealth by the price of Grosvenor's tobacco @ eight pence an ounce (YELL). Holmes makes reference to Watson's eternal tobacco (3STU, MUSG), cigars and tobacco are cited, and in MAZA pipes, cigars and tobacco are mentioned, yet no one is actually smoking in any of these stories.

The cases that are smoke-free are SUSS, DANC, BERY, and LION, meaning that there is no mention of anyone smoking, nor of pipes, cigars, cigarettes, or tobacco. In LION there is a reference to a butt but, it merely refers to Ian Murdoch possibly being the butt of practical jokes except that he looked so ferocious. Elias Openshaw (FIVE) smoked heavily; Holmes smoked hard (LADY), Hall Pycroft did a smoke (STOC), but we don't know what they smoked. Dr. Mortimer (HOUN) is the only character that actually made his own cigarettes and that, with surprising dexterity. Watson buys his cigarettes from Bradleys of Oxford Street (HOUN) and by not field stripping his discards allows Holmes to deduce he is in the hut on the moor. Holmes asks Culverton Smith for a cigarette, missing tobacco being so irksome (DYIN). Godfrey Emsworth (BLAN) lights a cigarette confident that it could hurt his health no more than a touch of leprosy. After he discarded his disguise as the old book seller and frightened poor Watson half to death, Holmes lit a cigarette in his old, nonchalant manner (EMPT). The strangest smoker of all was Thaddeus Sholto (SIGN) who smoked Eastern tobacco, with a balsamic odor, through a hookah, which proved to be an invaluable sedative. And then there are the cigars. John Turner smoked Indian cigars, rolled in Rotterdam (BOSC), as did Grimesby Roylott (SPEC). Our favorite non-Mormon from Utah, Jefferson Hope, smoked the most famous cigar of all, Trichonopoly, whose ash is dark in colour, flaky, and unique (STUD). Blessington (or Sutton) smoked Havanas, but his murderers, Biddle, Hayward and Moffat, smoked the peculiar sort of cigars that are imported by the Dutch from their East Indian colonies, usually wrapped in straw and thinner for their length than any other brand (RESI). Leon Sterndale (DEVI) smoked a perpetual cigar, and two major villains smoked cigars stuck out at an angle: Charles Augustus Milverton (CHAR) and Boss McGinty (VALL). Charles's cigar was long and black; McGinty's angle was acute. Altamont's cigar (LAST) was half-smoked and sodden and hung from the corner of his mouth. Jack Douglas sucked at his cigar (VALL), and Sir Charles Baskerville left a clue when he dropped his cigar ash twice (HOUN). There are several odd offers of cigars. Holmes asks Von Bork if he should light a cigar and place it between his lips. We don't know what the Dangling Prussian replied but it might have been a long, Teutonic curse (LAST). "Have a cigar," Holmes says to Jonathan Small after his capture (SIGN), and he has Watson give a nervous Jack Crocker a cigar, while he tells him to "bite on that" (ABBE). And Holmes, in his disguise as the aged, asthmatic seaman, with the perfect workhouse cough, says to Athelney Jones and Watson, "I think you might offer me a cigar" (SIGN). Other cigar smokers include Von Herling (LAST), Lestrade (SIXN), Tobias Gregson (STUD), and in many cases, Watson. Jabez Wilson takes snuff, according to Holmes's observations but he never actually takes it (REDH). Mycroft, though, does the snuff taking (GREE) as do Holmes and Watson. Or at least it sounds as if they do, as Holmes offers Watson a pinch from a snuffbox of old gold, with a great amethyst in the centre of the lid (IDEN). Snuff is mentioned again, but only once, as a description of the snuff-like powder residue of devils-foot root (DEVI). Chewing tobacco is cited in only one instance. Holmes deduces its presence on the letter received by Mrs. Neville St. Clair (TWIS). There are, remarkably, only two admitted non-smokers in all of the Canon and they are Percy Phelps (NAVA) and Sir James Damery (ILLU). Culverton Smith wore a smoking cap (DYIN). May we infer that he smoked? We just don't know. While most of the Canonical characters probably wound up in the lung cancer ward at St. Barts, only one character profited by their addictions and he was subject to peculiar persecution. I refer (cough, cough) to the well-known tobacco millionaire, John Vincent Harden (SOLI). A lot of people in the no-smoking section think it served him right.

Mea Culpa Canonica

I count eighty-eight instances of apologies, pardons, sorries, excuse-me's, or other offerings of regret in the Canon and perhaps, surprisingly, thirty-five per cent of them (31) emanate from that austere automaton, the positively inhuman calculating machine with the cold and proud nature, Mr. Sherlock Holmes. The most frequent recipient of his regrets (15) are, of course, the man he was closest to, Dr. Watson. To Watson, Holmes says, "excuse my rudeness," and "excuse my using your name" (STUD); "pray accept my apologies" (SIGN); "Excuse me, my dear fellow. I am sorry to make you a victim of what may seem a mere whim" (ABBE); "I must apologize for calling so late" (FINA); "You will excuse me for not waiting for you" (FIVE); "I'll just step in and see that kind gentleman, and tell him that if I was a bit gruff in my manner there was not any harm meant" and then a few moments later, "My dear Watson, I owe you a thousand apologies" and "I owe you many apologies" (EMPT). In SPEC Holmes says, "very sorry to knock you up;" in DYIN, "My dear Watson, I owe you a thousand apologies;" and in DANC, "As to you, my friend Watson, I owe you every atonement for having allowed your natural curiosity to remain so long unsatisfied." His most sincere apology occurs in DEVI when he almost causes the demise of both himself and his Boswell. "Upon my word, Watson!" said Holmes at last with an unsteady voice, "I owe you both my thanks and an apology. I am really very sorry." This incident answers the trivia question,

"Who came closest to killing off Holmes and Watson?" The answer is, of course, Holmes.

And the famous alleged misogynist apologizes, in some form, to the fair sex, on no less than six occasions, more then to any other group. To Mrs. Straker (SILV) "Ah, that quite settles it." With an apology he followed the inspector outside. To Mrs. Toller (COPP): "I am sure we owe you an apology." To the telegraph operator (MISS): "I am sorry to trouble you." To Lady Trelawney Hope (SECO): "I am sorry for you Lady Hilda." To Irene Adler, in the disguise of the old clergyman (SCAN), "I rose, and, making my excuses, escaped from the house." To Lady Brackenstall (ABBE), "I am sorry."

He apologizes to police officers three times. "I really must apologize, Hopkins, I fear the scrambled eggs are cold" (BLAC); and to Lestrade, "I really beg your pardon" (STUD). In (REIG), after feigning illness, with a shamefaced apology for his weakness," and later, "I was sorry to cause you the sympathetic pain which I know that you felt." Inspector Forrester is among the recipients of this. Holmes apologizes to a doctor (Leslie Armstrong, MISS), to a professor (Presbury, CREE), to a convict (Jonathan Small, SIGN), to a foreign office clerk (Percy Phelps, NAVA), to an heir (Sir Henry Baskerville, HOUN), to a discreet intermediary (Sir James Damery, ILLU) and to a pawnbroker (Jabez Wilson; REDH). To Dr. Leslie Armstrong: "Excuse me, I think we are a little at cross-purposes (MISS)," to Professor Presbury: "I am sorry, Professor, but the matter was rather confidential"(CREE). "To our favorite convict, "Well, Jonathan Small, I am sorry that it has come to this (SIGN)," to Percy Phelps, he said soothingly "There, there, It was too bad to spring it on you like this (NAVA)." To Sir Henry, "We owe you a deep apology for having exposed you to this fright (HOUN)." To Sir James Damery, "Then you will excuse me if I light my pipe (ILLU)," and "I am sorry. I am accustomed to having mystery at one end of my cases, but to have it at both ends is confusion (SECO)." To Jabez Wilson, "But there is, if you will excuse my saying so, something just a little funny about it" (REDH) .

And Holmes suggests that others apologize, too. "You owe a very humble apology to that noble lad, your son" (to Alexander Holder, BERYL), and to Stanley Hopkins (BLAC), "I confess that I think you owe him [John Hopley Neligan] some apology."

On the receiving end, Holmes hears Lord Robert St. Simon beg his pardon twice (NOBL), and Colonel Ross, somewhat shamefully, tells Holmes, "I owe you a thousand apologies for having doubted your ability" (SILV). In NORW we hear, "I'm sorry, Mr. Holmes, I am the unhappy John Hector McFarlane." Thorneycroft Huxtable (PRIO) barges in to 221B and after fainting, croaks, "Forgive this weakness, Mr. Holmes." Cecil Barker offers, "Sorry to interrupt your consultation," (VALL), and Cartwright wires Holmes, "Visited twenty-three hotels as directed but sorry to report unable to trace cut sheet of Times" (HOUN).

Two arch villains try to be polite, but Baron Gruner's (ILLU) apology is tinged with malice, "Excuse my amusement, Mr. Holmes, but it is really funny to see you trying to play a hand with no cards in it." The serpent-like Charles Augustus Milverton (CHAS) "...advanced with a plump little hand extended, murmuring his regret for having missed us at his first visit." Of course, Holmes refuses this plump little hand.

Other apologies follow: Trevor Bennett: "I am so sorry, Mr. Holmes. I wished to apologize" (CREE); the King of Bohemia, "You will excuse this mask" (SCAN), and Mr. Merryweather, "Really, Mr. Holmes... I do not know how the bank can thank you or repay you" (REDH). James Windibank, after saying "Yes, sir. I am afraid I'm a little late" adds, "I am sorry that Miss Sutherland has troubled you about this little matter;"(IDEN), and Violet Hunter says, "You will excuse my troubling you, I am sure (COPP). Inspector Gregory laments "I am sorry to say we have made very little progress (SILV), and Mr. Sandeford of Reading says, "Yes, sir, I fear that I am a little late, but the trains were awkward (SIXN).

Holmes, together with Watson, was on the receiving end of many apologies: "I owe you an apology;" (John Openshaw, FIVE); "I beg your pardon," said he, "with some embarrassment;" (Grant Munro, YELL); with Hall Pycroft, "If I might trespass upon your patience so far (Harry Pinner, STOC); and with Percy Trevelyan, "...I am sorry if my precautions have annoyed you" (Blessington, RESI).

Watson, by himself, hears many an apology, too. "You will, I am sure, excuse my presumption" (Stapleton, HOUN); "I wanted to say to you how sorry I am about the stupid mistake I made in thinking you were Sir Henry" (Beryl Stapleton HOUN);

The stranger held out a huge, sunburned hand with a few words of apology (Philip Green, LADY); "I am sorry to knock you up so early, Doctor" (Victor Hatherley, ENGR); to Watson and his Mrs., we hear, "You will excuse my calling so late" (Kate Whitney, TWIS), and then in the same case, "You will, I am sure, forgive anything that may be wanting in our arrangements, when you consider the blow which has come so suddenly upon us" (Mrs. Neville St. Clair, TWIS).

And the good doctor also offers apologies. To Holmes, "I regret the injustice which I did you" (SIGN); to Holmes and Jabez Wilson, "With an apology for my intrusion, I was about to withdraw" (REDH); to Holmes and Mary Morstan, "You will, I am sure, excuse me" (SIGN); and to Ivy Douglas and Cecil Barker, "And so, I will beg leave to resume my walk." (VALL). The most poignant statement comes from Harold Stackhurst who says to Ian Murdoch, "Forgive what is past..." (LION), and the phoniest comes from the phony Russian nobleman in RESI, when he says to Percy Trevelyan, "I feel I owe you a great many apologies for my abrupt departure yesterday, Doctor." The least sincere apology comes from Culverton Smith (DYIN) when he hears that Holmes is dying: "I am sorry to hear this." In SIGN, Williams says to Mary Morstan, "You will excuse me Miss," and later on, McMurdo, the guard, explains, "Very sorry, Mr. Thaddeus," twice. Mary Morstan had already told Thaddeus, "You will excuse me, Mr. Sholto." Robert St. Simon tells Hattie Doran, bitterly, "Pray make no apology to me." Later she counters with, "I am very sorry if I have given you pain," and he replies, "Excuse me, but it is not my custom to discuss my most intimate personal affairs in this public manner" (NOBL). There are a lot of apologies in VALL, more than in any other case and Bodymaster McGinty is on the receiving end most of the time. John McMurdo says, "I'm sorry Councillor, I'm strange to the ways of the place," and "I should apologize. I spoke without thought." McGinty hears from his bartender, "I'm sorry, Councillor, but it's Ted Baldwin," and poor apologetic Morris, the "nicest" of the Scowrers, apologizes to both McGinty and McMurdo respectively. "I apologize Eminent Bodymaster," and "I am sorry I gave you the trouble to come and meet me." McMurdo receives one apology from a policeman, "No offense, stranger," and another from the Freeman, Scanlan, "All right, mate, no offense meant." And, surprisingly, he offers an apology to sour-faced Ted Baldwin, "It's all over for me and I bear no grudge," for which he receives nothing but a sullen look in return.

Three apologies are merely referred to. Alexander Holder tells Holmes "I must fly to my dear boy to apologize to him for the wrong which I have done him" (BERY); Violet Smith says, "Mr. Carruthers apologized to me next day" (SOLI) and Sir Henry comments to Dr. Watson, "I must allow that no man could make a more handsome apology than he [Stapleton] has done (HOUN). The most sinister remark comes from the devil himself, the sailor, Hudson, when he tells Trevor Senior, "I've not had my 'pology." We all know what happens then. Actually, we don't know, do we? (GLOR).

Sorry about that.

Dr. Watson's Wound Pension

Veterans Administration
14A Downing Street
London, U.K.

June 1, 1901
Dr. John H. Watson
221B Baker Street
London

Dear Sir,

We are responding to your request for an increase in your wound pension. An examination of the records indicate that you were shot by the murderous Ghazis during the second Afghan war at the Battle of Maiwand. Your injury, a Jezail bullet in your shoulder which shattered the bone and grazed the subclavian artery, has been authenticated.

However, where our application requests the location of the wound you filled in: "either my shoulder or my leg." This is most unsatisfactory. When an army veteran forgets where he has been wounded we feel he needs help of some sort. We understand fully that as we age we become more and more forgetful but not knowing where you were wounded seems an extreme case. Therefore, we feel you should make an appointment with an alienist (we recommend a Doctor S. Freud), or at least a physical therapist, who can explain to you which is your arm and which is your leg.

In addition, we have heard from sources that have proved reliable in the past, that you have been squandering your current wound pension on the turf. If this is indeed the case (and we have a well known private detective to investigate) we will be unable to pay you more money. We can only offer wound pensions to veterans who meet our high moral standards.

God Save the Queen.

J.Wimpy Wellington
Department of Wounds
Veterans Administration

Queen Victoria and Neutrality During the American Civil War

Britannia Rules the Waves but Britannia Waives the Rules

The American Civil War began at 4:30 a.m. on April 12, 1861 with Confederate forces firing on Union-held Fort Sumter, in Charleston, South Carolina. Just a month later, on May 13, Queen Victoria issued a proclamation commanding British subjects to observe the provisions of the Foreign Enlistment Act of 1818 that prohibited Britons from joining the army or navy of any belligerent, from arming or equipping any ship for use as a ship of war or military transport, from breaking any lawful blockade, and from carrying "officers, soldiers, dispatches, arms, military stores of material" and other contraband to any belligerent. For the four years of the American Civil War England violated most of these prohibitions.

Union General Winfield Scott introduced the Anaconda Plan, a blockade of Southern ports that would keep their cotton from being shipped out and war materiel from coming in. Britain even recognized Confederate belligerency, which meant that ships flying the Confederate flag were treated in British ports like ships of any belligerent nation. Under rules established by international law, ships of belligerents were allowed to obtain fuel, supplies and repairs in neutral ports but could not obtain additional equipment or armament. The royal proclamation permitted the Confederate cruisers that would ravage Northern shipping to obtain vital supplies and coal during visits to British colonial ports. This was not neutrality. Britain held back, however, from recognizing the Confederate States as a national entity. Had they done so, Secretary of State William Henry Seward thundered, it would equate to an act of war.

The Confederate States of America began life with no navy and few facilities for creating one. Its navy would be built in British shipyards. For the sensitive task of exploiting this source Confederate Secretary of the Navy Stephen Mallory, selected James. D. Bulloch of Georgia. James and his sister, Martha, grew up in Bulloch Hall, an estate just outside of Atlanta. It is said that a newspaper reporter visited Bulloch Hall in the 1920s and liked what she saw. Her name was Margaret Mitchell who wrote Gone With the Wind. Martha married a New Yorker named Theodore Roosevelt. They had two sons, Theodore, Jr. and Elliot. Future president Teddy Roosevelt's uncle Jim would buy ships for the Confederate navy and Elliot's daughter, Anna Eleanor, would marry a man named Franklin Delano Roosevelt.

Arriving in Liverpool in June 1861, Bulloch quickly signed contracts for two steam/sail cruisers that eventually became the famed commerce raiders Florida and Alabama. These British-built raiders represented an important part of Confederate naval strategy. In any war, enemy merchant shipping becomes fair game. The Confederates sent armed raiders to roam the oceans in search of northern vessels. The two hundred and ninetieth ship (it was referred to as the 290) built by the Laird Brothers of Birkenhead, near Liverpool, became the Alabama, soon to be captained by Raphael Semmes. The Alabama destroyed or captured 64 American merchant ships before being sunk by the USS Kearsarge off Cherbourg in June 1864, an incident commemorated by the French artist, Manet. Dreading this elusive raider and others, Northern ship owners either laid their vessels up or transferred them to foreign flags. In 1860, 2/3rds of the commerce of New York was carried in American bottoms, but by 1863 3/4's of it came in foreign ships, mostly British. Obviously, England was profiteering from the American Civil War.

The Alabama was not the only Confederate ship to sail from a British port. Besides the Florida, the Rappahannock, and the Georgia, the Shenandoah provided an ironic postscript to the war by refusing to surrender after Appomattox, in April 1865, and burning a large part of the American whaling fleet in the Bering Sea during the early summer of that year. The Confederate commerce raiders were the best known but not the only example of the unneutral British acts, and Britain's friendliness toward the South infuriated the Union. Prime Minister Lord Palmerston and his government seemed to shut its eyes to violations of British neutrality by Liverpool shipbuilders who constructed rebel cruisers to prey on American merchant marine. The British subscribed heavily to the Confederate cotton loan and blockade-runners set out from the Mersey, the Clyde and the Thames rivers in the hundreds. England's interpretation of the neutrality laws converted Nassau, in the Bahamas, into an insurgent port, which could not be blockaded by the naval forces of the United States. From the safety of Canada, Southern agents seized shipping on the Great Lakes and in November 1864 shot up the town of St. Albans, Vermont, and robbed three banks before disappearing over the border to be arrested briefly before being released by a flagrantly biased judge.

"The great body of the aristocracy and the wealthy commercial classes," wrote American minister Charles Francis Adams, "are anxious to see the United States go to pieces." Despite American diplomats' prodigious efforts in gathering the most damning evidence, British official tardiness and narrow interpretation of the letter of the law meant that the Confederate cruisers escaped from British ports with ease. No matter how often Britain had infringed the spirit of their neutrality statutes the commerce raiders were nearly always welcome at British colonial ports and passengers on British ships cheered the Alabama as she passed. Finally, in 1863, Adams, in order to stop Laird rams from sailing presented an ultimatum that went to the brink of war. These ironclad rams had an iron bar at their prow and would have proved deadly to the wooden blockading squadron. And after the twin Union victories at Gettysburg and Vicksburg, England listened at last, albeit slowly. Legally, they still could not stop the manufacture of these dangerous vessels so they bought them for the English navy. The Confederates were infuriated and historians agree that if these rams reached America the Civil War might have turned out differently.

The British government allegedly did try to do its duty as it saw it, but it was hamstrung by a law which drew a fine distinction between building a vessel and equipping it for war. The Confederate raiders, built as warships but supplied with guns and shells <u>outside</u> the British jurisdiction in, for example, the Azores, were immune. But here were ships built with British materials by British workmen and manned largely by trained gunners of the British Naval Reserve putting into British colonial parts for supplies and repairs and then sailing out to overhaul and destroy one Union merchantman after another. This was not neutrality.

In 1871, a joint High Commission was established to settle war time disputes between America, Britain and Canada. The board consisted of five members, one each from America, England, Brazil, Italy and Switzerland. They met in Geneva in what was the first great tribune of arbitration. The <u>Alabama</u> Claims - the American demands for compensation from Great Britain for unneutral acts during the Civil War - were not settled for seven years after the end of the fighting and relations between the two countries were gravely strained by the negotiations. Much to Britain's chagrin, the High Commission awarded America $15.5 million, or 3.2 million pounds, for violating Britain's pledge of neutrality and helping the Confederates during the Great War of the Rebellion, as the Civil War is officially known.

England paid the claims in 1873.

Little Known Facts About Well Known Canon Characters

Abrahams (LADY) - Although once in mortal terror of his life, he recovered well enough to be able to win the 440 in the 1924 Olympics, featured in the movie <u>Chariots of Fire</u>.

Agatha (CHAS) - After being jilted by the plumber Escott, she left the Milverton household and began to write murder mysteries for a living.

Bannister (3STU) - Servant to Hilton Soames and first man to run a mile in less than four minutes.

John Barrymore (HOUN) - After Selden's funeral he and Eliza went to Hollywood where people commented on his great profile.

Mrs. Bernstone (SIGN) - Housekeeper to Bartholomew Sholto. Her son, Leonard, wrote the music for <u>West Side Story</u>.

Miss Burnet (WIST) - Governess of Don Murillo's children, she starred in Broadway's <u>Moon Over Buffalo</u>.

Lal Chowdar (SIGN) - After Thaddeus Sholto's death, he married an Irish woman and modeled men's clothing. People always wondered who put the overalls on Mrs. Murphy's Chowdar.

Joyce Cummings (THOR) - The first barrister to be listed in Who's Who in English Women.

James Desmond (HOUN) - Next in line to inherit the Baskerville fortune in the event of Sir Henry's death. His sister Norma lived on Sunset Boulevard.

White Mason (VALL) and Steve Dixie (3GAB) went into business manufacturing men's monogrammed boxing shorts. Buyers flocked to see the new Mason-Dixon line.

Ray Ernest (RETI) - Murdered chess-playing neighbor of Josiah Amberley. Oscar Wilde wrote his biography, The Importance of Being Ernest.

Jefferson Hope (STUD) - During his travels in America he met Abner Doubleday in Cooperstown, N.Y. and helped him lay out the plans for the infield in the game of baseball. Doubleday always called that idea the Hope Diamond.

Abdullah Khan (SIGN) - One nephew Ali, married Rita Hayworth; another, Sammy, wrote music for Frank Sinatra.

Isadora Klein (3GAB) - Her adventures with Douglas Maberley was turned into the musical, Eine Kleine Nacht Musik.

Lestrade - Best known Scotland Yarder. Vittoria De Sica made a movie of his life, La Strada, starred Anthony Quinn and Giulietta Messina.

H. Lowenstein of Prague (CREE) - His son, Laszlo, was creepy, too. He became a movie star under the name of Peter Lorre, whose real name was Laszlo Lowenstein.

Teddy Marvin (VALL) - Gaining the monopoly on flowers in Vermissa Valley, he soon became famous for his lawn decorations, known as Marvin Gardens.

Charles McCarthy (BOSC) - Blackmailer of John Turner. A chance meeting with Edgar Bergen changed his life.

Mortimer (GOLD) - Professor Coram's gardener and country cousin of Charles McCarthy.

Jackson (CROO) - Watson's accommodating physician neighbor. He and his partners founded the first English Health Maintenance Organization called Clayton, Jackson and Durante.

Alec MacDonald (VALL) - He consulted Holmes in the Birlstone murder case prior to entering the fast-food business with his son, Ronald.

Mrs. Marker (GOLD - Petite housekeeper to Professor Coram. Her father once left her in lieu of a gambling debt, as shown in the movie, Little Miss Marker, starring Shirley Temple and Adolph Menjou.

Mary Jane (SCAN) - Watson's incorrigible servant girl. Given notice by Mrs. Watson she grew a controlled substance in her back yard which was eventually named after her.

Lord Mount-James (MISS) - After cutting Godfrey Staunton out of his will, he asked Sherlock Holmes to look into the bank-robbing activities of his two other nephews, Jesse and Frank Mount-James.

Grant Munro (YELL) - He issued a caveat to all Englishmen to have more trust in their wives. This became known as the Munro Doctrine.

Spencer John Gang (3GAB) - So named because of its peculiar modus operandi of robbing elderly gentlemen in the loo.

Robert St. Simon (NOBL) - Noble bachelor formerly associated with folk singer Art St. Garfunkle.

Cadogan West (BRUC) - Mae's second son, murdered by Hugo Oberstein with a lifesaver. Lifesavers, or lifejackets, are now known as Mae Wests.

Theresa Wright (ABBE) - The personal maid of Lady Mary Fraser Brackenstall. After Mary's marriage to Jack Croker, she left for Hollywood where she appeared in the movie Shadow of a Doubt with Joseph Cotton.

To Tell the Truth

Rogets's <u>Thesaurus</u>, under the headings "falseness, exaggeration and deception, numbers 354, 355 and 356, respectively, have over 500 variations of untruthfulness, a.k.a. the lie. Some are fancy: meretricious and specious; others simple: fib and stretch the truth. And so many Canonical characters were meretricious. They fibbed; they lied; they stretched the truth. And some of those fibs and lies and stretchings, with apologies to Burger King, were whoppers. Some lived a lie, like Birdy Edwards (VALL), Trevor, Sr. (GLOR), John Clay (REDH), Von Bork and Altamont (LAST), James Windibank as Hosmer Angel (IDEN), Blessington (RESI), Neville St. Clair (TWIS), John Garrideb (3GAR), the Stapletons (HOUN), Holy Peters (LADY) and Miss Burnet (WIST). Some lied to save their skins, like Colonel Valentine Walter (BRUC), Josiah Amberley (RETI), Mary Holder (BERY), Mortimer Tregennis (DEVI), James Ryder (BLUE), Joseph Harrison (NAVA), the Cunninghams, pere et fils (REIG), and Jack Croker, Lady Brackenstall and Theresa Wright (ABBE). Bob Carruthers and Roaring Jack Woodley lied to gain a fortune through a phony marriage (SOLI); Major Sholto lied to gain the Agra treasure (SIGN); Baron Gruner lied to gain a fiancée (ILLU); Colonel Barclay lied to rid himself of a rival (CROO); Sir Robert Norberton created a lie so as to hide the death of his sister (SHOS), and Achmet, the unhappy merchant, lied about his "iron box which contains one or two little family matters which are of no value to others"(SIGN). Some lied to protect loved ones: Colonel

Emsworth (BLAN), Bannister the butler (3STU), Elsie Patrick Cubitt, (DANC), Lady Trelawney Hope (SECO), Barrymore (HOUN), Dr. Leslie Armstrong (MISS), Effie Munro (YELL), Ivy Douglas, together with Cecil James Barker (VALL), and Professor Coram (GOLD). J. Neil Gibson (THOR) and the King of Bohemia (SCAN) lied to fend off embarrassment and Gibson's lack of candor nearly caused the death of an innocent woman. Harold Latimer's lies came close to costing the Greek interpreter his life (GREE). Jonas Oldacre's mendacity almost caused an asthmatic, bachelor, Freemason, solicitor to lose his freedom (NORW) and Lysander Stark's lie regarding fuller's earth cost a hydraulic engineer his thumb (ENGR). Holmes created a fictitious persona, Dr. Hill Barton, so that Watson could lie to Baron Gruner about his expertise with Ming Dynasty egg-shell saucers (ILLU) and "Mrs. Sawyer" lied to gain back a precious wedding band for Jefferson Hope (STUD).

And talk about fabrications. The phony Russian nobleman's "son" lied about his "father's" catatonic spells for the benefit of Dr. Percy Trevelyan (RESI). And under the heading of creative thinking, Arthur Pinner (or was it Harry?) envisioned the Franco-Midland Hardware Company just for Hall Pycroft (STOC), while John Clay invented the Red Headed League for Jabez Wilson (REDH).

But the dissimulation and misleading behavior of the aforementioned characters pale next to the disingenuous world of the world's foremost consulting detective. Sherlock Holmes lied, as the saying goes, like a rug. "Surely we have met before" (SILV); "I am an accountant" to Watson's "a clerk" (STOC); "I can hardly put my foot on the ground," (PRIO); "I am liable for these sudden nervous attacks" (REIG); "I heard through a second person that Professor Presbury of Camford had need of my services"(CREE); "I am a dog fancier myself (SHOS); "I am a neighbor of yours for you'll find my little bookshop at the corner of Church Street"(EMPT); "I am a plumber with a rising business, Escott by name" (CHAS); "I forgot to put my name on the telegram (MISS); I am returning to London tomorrow" (HOUN), "I found myself mumbling responses which were whispered in my ear, and vouching for things of which I knew nothing (SCAN); and to cap it off, his whole performance in DYIN.

Did Holmes ever write a trifling monograph on disinformation? He had as much experience with that as with cigar ashes and tattoos.

Two characters actually accuse Holmes of lying and one gets it right. Silas Brown listens as Holmes whispers in his ear and then "He started violently and flushed to the temples. 'It's a lie,' he shouted" (SILV). On this occasion, though, Holmes is telling the truth. In SOLI, Holmes said, "In the first place, three of you came from South Africa on this game – you Williamson, you Carruthers, and Woodley."

"Lie number one," said the old man, "I never saw either of them until two months ago, and I have never been in Africa in my life, so you can put that in your pipe and smoke it, Mr. Busybody Holmes." Technically speaking, Holmes didn't lie. He was just mistaken, a rarity in itself.

I would think there are even more falsehoods in the Canon but the aforementioned should do for now. And that, with my hand on the Bible, is the truth, the whole truth, and nothing but the truth. So help me, God.

Sherlock Holmes' Most Infamous Cousin

Sherlock Holmes was certainly reticent regarding his family. We learn of his brother. Mycroft, only in GREE. But there were other reasons, too. Sherlock had an uncle, Wendell Oliver Holmes, Siger Holmes' much older brother. Oliver had only one child, a precocious but headstrong daughter, Mary Ann, and there was a very good reason why Holmes never spoke of her. After a splendid education and a rigorous upbringing, Mary Ann, a highly individualistic adventuress, rebelled and left the family forever. It was not easy for a young woman to make any sort of a living then and she ended up, like Liza Doolittle, selling flowers outside Covent Garden Theater. Like Liza (George Bernard Shaw was aware of Mary Ann's history when he wrote <u>Pygmalion</u>) Mary Ann was a diamond-in-the-rough beauty, and a well-known actor, after buying up her flowers day after day, expressed his love for her. He was so infatuated with Mary Ann that he took her to America with him for a Shakespearean tour, and a fraudulent, on stage, marriage.

He neglected to mention that he already had a wife and child in London.

In America, he continued to perform and they had a large family, settling in Bel Air, Maryland. Unhappily, all of their children were illegitimate. Three of their sons became famous actors. Edwin, John, and Junius, Jr. John's middle name came from a famous English orator who championed America in Parliament during the Revolutionary war. He was so pro-

American that the colonists named a city after him in Pennsylvania. After the death of her husband, Mary Ann moved to New York City where she lived on East 17th Street. All through the Civil War her sons John and Edwin visited her. John was enamored with the Confederate way of life but Edwin was a staunch Unionist. Mary Ann's home was neutral ground; they never argued in front of their mother.

You see, Mary Ann Holmes had married Junius Booth, the great tragedian, had a son named John Wilkes Booth (that city in Pennsylvania is Wilkes-Barre) and her son killed one of the greatest presidents in American history. And that is why neither Sherlock or Mycroft ever mentioned her.

The facts are these: John Wilkes Booth's mother was indeed Mary Ann Holmes and she sold flowers in Covent Gardens. She really did come to America with Junius Booth, who was married and had a son. All of their children were illegitimate and she did live at 107 East 17th Street just across the street from Washington Irving. His house stands; hers does not. John and Edwin Booth visited her frequently but they never argued in her presence. Her house is a stop on my famous tour of New York City and the Civil War.

Chapter 3

Canonical Body Parts

Getting A Head

We have a quartet of hairless Canonical heads: the broad bald head of Baron Von Herling (LAST), the high bald head of Culverton Smith (DYIN), and the bald, shining scalps of Thaddeus and Bartholomew Sholto (SIGN). Charles Augustus Milverton had a broad, large, intellectual, grizzled head, with a shining patch of baldness, and his killer wore a diamond tiara upon her noble head (CHAS). Professor Presbury's head was grizzled (CREE), Steve Dixie's was wooly (3GAB), Henry Baker's was massive (BLUE), Tonga's was great and misshapen (SIGN), and the cockroach killer from the Copper Beeches, Edward Rucastle, had a head disproportionately large (COPP). Lady Trelawney Hope had the nicest head in the Canon. Hers was exquisite with beautiful coloring (SECO).

Among foreheads mentioned, we have Colonel Sebastian Moran, who had a high, bald forehead (EMPT), Holmes, whose forehead had a discolored lump (SOLI), and Leon Sterndale, who had knotted passionate veins in his (DEVI). The man with the most interesting forehead of all, the fourth smartest man in London, and possibly the third most daring, John Clay (of royal birth), had a white splash of acid upon his forehead, just as Holmes had predicted (REDH).

He was ahead of his time.

The Mystery of The Grey-Eyed Men (And Women)

Perhaps Sir Arthur Conan Doyle's pregnant mother was frightened by a grey-eyed man.

Why else would not only Sherlock Holmes, but also his murderous arch-enemies, (Professor Moriarty, Culverton Smith, Charles Augustus Milverton), bellicose characters (J. Neil Gibson and Professor Presbury), and his brother, Mycroft, all have grey eyes? The famous mathematics coach had eyes deeply sunk in his head (FINA); the authority on obscure Asiatic diseases had two sullen, menacing eyes (DYIN); and the well-known blackmailer's eyes were keen, restless and penetrating (CHAS). The American senator had eyes that were cold and resentful (THOR), and the man who sought eternal youth through monkey glands, had a pair of keen, intense eyes, observant and clever to the verge of cunning (CREE). All were grey.

But that's not all. John Douglas's grey eyes were both keen and bold (VALL); his alter-ego, John McMurdo, had grey eyes that alternated from being humorous, to gleaming with sudden and dangerous anger (VALL); Wilson Kemp's ocular equipment was steel grey and they glistened coldly with a malignant inexorable cruelty in their depth (GREE); Thorneycroft Huxtable's grey eyes were vacant (PRIO); Dr. James Mortimer had two keen grey eyes (HOUN); Mrs. Rucastle's were light grey (COPP), and Colonel Lysander Stark's were not only grey but also bright

(ENGR). Miss Burnet, the unfortunate governess of the Tiger of San Pedro's offspring, while drugged, had pupils that were dark dots in the centre of the broad, grey iris (WIST); villain Jonas Oldacre saw things through keen, shifty, light grey eyes (NORW), and that most tactful of men, Colonel Sir James Damery, had grey Irish eyes (ILLU).

Sherlock Holmes' eyes were variously described as mischievous (MUSG); gleaming (BRUC); quick (THOR); clear, hard (3GAR), and steady; like two menacing points of steel (MAZA). They had a dreamy, vacant lacklustre expression; were sharp and piercing, and fairly glittered (STUD). They shone brightly between puckered lids; and were languid, dreamy (REDH). They had the brightness of fever, and shone more brightly out of darker hollows (DYIN). They danced with amusement (HOUN), and they were shining like stars (NORW). His dull eyes had regained their fire (TWIS); he had a twinkle of a smile in his eyes, and they became keen and dark in his disguise as an aged seafaring man (SIGN). They were deep-set and inscrutable (MISS); keen and deep-set (ABBE), and as bright and keen as rapiers (RETI). And they were grey (HOUN, RETI, THOR, MAZA). Brother Mycroft had peculiarly light watery grey eyes (GREE). Or were they steel-grey and deep set (BRUC)?

Holmes undoubtedly had more ocular descriptions than anyone else in the Canon and the color "grey" almost nudges out "dark" as Doyle's favorite visual hue. References to "dark" run almost 29%, and by contrast, "grey" is 27%, "blue" 26%, and "black" 12%. As the notable exceptions to these shades, only Lucy Ferrier (STUD), and Eugenia Ronder (VEIL), have brown eyes,

Alice Turner (BOSC) had violet eyes, and both Sir Henry Baskerville and Laura Lyons (HOUN) had eyes of the hazel variety.

Statistically speaking, I would think that blue eyes predominated among English citizens, especially during Sherlock Holmes' life. Why then are there so many grey-eyed men and women in his adventures?

Just a moment. Hum. I have been as blind as a mole. Let us turn to page seven of The Annotated Sherlock Holmes, edited, with an introduction, notes and bibliography by William S. Baring-Gould. It reads as follows:

"Conan Doyle set out to create a private detective who would not fail in such an assignment because he would have developed habits of observation and inference into a system, and he thought at once of one of his former teachers at the University, Joseph Bell, M.D....A thin, wiry, dark man, with a high-nosed acute face, penetrating GREY EYES, angular shoulders and a high discordant voice. Dr. Bell would sit in his receiving room with a face like a Red Indian and diagnose the people as they came in, before they even opened their mouths."

Dr. John H. Watson, late of the Indian Army, who showed an unresponsive eye (VALL), and a surgical eye (SUSS), but never one with color in it, might have said to Holmes, "Elementary!"

Legs, Limbs and Feet

There are several amputees mentioned in the Canon, and one is an American Civil War general. Jonathan Small (SIGN), Francis Prosper (BERY), and the one-legged new vendor (ILLU) stomped around on wooden legs, while spindled-legged Josiah Amberley used an artificial limb (RETI). The real-life wooden legger was none other than Confederate General John B. Hood, who had once commanded Elias Openshaw during America's Civil War (FIVE). Hood lost his right leg at the battle of Chickamauga in September 1863.

Both Sherlock Holmes (COPP, NOBL) and James Stanger (VALL), had long, thin legs. John Turner (BOSC) was strong of limb even though he limped with the right leg and the phony cataleptic visiting Dr. Percy Trevelyan (RESI) had a "son" who had the limbs (and chest) of a Hercules. Big Bob Ferguson was loose-limbed (SUSS), poor John Hopley Nelligan shook in every limb (BLAC), and Harraway of the Scowrers had nervous, jerky limbs (VALL).

Re the appendages at the end of those Canonical limbs, Jefferson Hope's feet differed from those of Abe Slaney's even though they were both big men. Hope (STUD) had small feet, and the most dangerous crook in Chicago had large masculine feet, with peculiarly long, sharp toes (DANC). Blessington (RESI) had ungainly feet, Inspector Lestrade's left foot had an inward twist (BOSC), Holmes, disguised as an opium addict had an uncertain foot (TWIS), and Cartwright of the Express office had a very active pair of feet (HOUN).

The most famous limb of all still had a Jezail bullet in it. But which limb? (STUD, NOBL). Dr. Watson seemed to have forgotten.

Fingers, Fists and Nails

ACD had a thing about long, thin fingers, particularly when it came to his roommate. Holmes' fingers are cold and thin (EMPT), long and thin (REDC, SILV), long and sensitive (THOR), and long and nervous (LADY). James Ryder (BLUE) has quivering fingers as does Dr. Mortimer (HOUN), whose fingers are not only long and quivering but as agile and restless as the antennae of an insect, agile enough to be able to roll his own cigarettes. Mrs. Sawyer (STUD) has nervous, shaky fingers, and Mrs. Bernstone (SIGN) has restless, picking fingers. Holmes produces a cautionary forefinger (3GAB), Watson exhibits a right forefinger black with nitrate of silver (SCAN), and Violet Smith (SOLI) has the spatulate finger ends of a musician (or a typist). Both Jack Croker (ABBE) and the Master have the best of all possible fingers, Croker's being very dexterous and Holmes' being exceptionally strong (BERY).

A word or two about those fingers folding into fists, both innocent and baleful. Lucy Ferrier (STUD) had speckled, dimpled fists, while J. Neil Gibson's (THOR) were great and knotted and Steve Dixie's (3GAB) were huge, lumpy and knotted. Canonical nails are rarely mentioned. Laura Lyons' (HOUN) pink nails turned white on hearing that Jack Stapleton had betrayed her, and Jefferson Hope had remarkably long fingernails, at least on his right hand as we all know.

Rache lives.

Vox Populi

Three Canonical characters's voices are in the high range: Culverton Smith (high, petulant and penetrating; also high and screaming, DYIN); Jonathan Small (high and cracked, SIGN); and Professor Presbury (high, screaming; also with a strange, shrill falsetto, CREE). Four are deep voiced: Mary Morstan (deep and rich, SIGN); Sam Merton (deep and raucous, MAZA); Big Bob Ferguson (deep and hearty; also hoarse, SUSS); and Lord Holdernesse (PRIO), whose deep sonorous voice boomed out like a dinner-gong. BONGGGGG. John McMurdo (VALL) had a fine tenor voice, and Jack Douglas (VALL), his Doppelganger, did him one better by having a remarkably rich tenor voice. Sir James Damery (ILLU) had pleasant mellow voice, but so, in a way, did Baron Adelbert Gruner, the Austrian murderer, (ILLU) who had a silky voice, a gentle voice and an engaging voice. Another charmer, Charles Augustus Milverton (CHAS), had a smooth and suave voice. And to round off a trio of sweet-voiced horrors, we have the Reverend Shlessinger (LADY) who had an unctuous, make-everything-easy voice. Holmes had a weak voice (ILLU), a croaking and spasmodic voice (DYIN), and a strange, croaking voice in his disguise as the strange, old book collector (EMPT). Beryl Stapleton (HOUN) had a curious lisp, and also a thrill in her voice; Nathan Garrideb (3GAR) had a thin, quavering voice as did Mr. Blessington (RESI), whose quavering voice was also reedy. Lord Mount James' (MISS) voice was querulous, with a sharp crackle, and Harold Latimer (GREE) had a rasping way of saying words. Athelney Jones (SIGN) had a husky and confident voice, and the baleful Guiseppe Gorgiano's (REDC) voice boomed like thunder. The most interesting Canonical voice though, belongs to Violet DeMerville (ILLU). Her voice was like the wind from an iceberg.

That's enough to give anyone the shivers.

Beards

We have a great many beards in the Canon with black, short, and bristling, the most common. Out of a total of 40 bearded men 10 are in the ebony category including: Mr. Melas (GREE), Barrymore (square, HOUN), Eustace Brackenstall (short, ABBE), Boss McGinty (VALL), Abe Slaney (bristling, DANC), Philip Green (bristling, LADY), and Peter Carey (huge, BLAC). All of our disguised characters have black beards: Arthur Pinner (STOC), Jack Stapleton (bushy, HOUN), and Bob Carruthers (short, coal black, SOLI). Gennaro Luccas' (REDC) whiskers are dark but not black.

Those who have beards with no particular description are: Jefferson Hope (STUD), Rodger Prescott (alias Waldron, 3GAR), Mr. Kent (BLAN), Jonathan Small (SIGN), Mr. Fowler (COPP), and Mr. Menzies, the Scotsman (VALL).

Herr Heidegger's (PRIO) beard is full, and our favorite convict, Selden (HOUN), has a beard that in life is bristly but in death it is dripping.

Colonel Emsworth's (BLAN) beard is grey and straggling, and among the denizens of the Valley of Fear, Lawler has a ragged, grizzled beard, and Harraway is known as old greybeard. The litigious Mr. Frankland (HOUN) has grey whiskers that bristle, and Godfrey Staunton's (MISS) visitor has a grizzled beard. Mr. Ferguson (ENGR) has a chinchilla beard growing out of the creases of his double chin. How about that?

Our brindled beards belong to Peter Carey (BLAC) and Leon Sterndale (DEVI). Brindled means grey or tawny with darker streaks or spots. Yet earlier, we learn that Sterndale has a golden beard, at least at the fringes, yet white near the lips, and Black Peter's beard we know is black. I guess beards change color in different lights.

White beards include our defrocked clergyman Mr. Williamson (whose beard is also described as grey, SOLI), and Professor Coram's (GOLD) white beard is stained yellow around the mouth.

Our red beards (Barbarossa, the code name for Hitler's invasion of Russia) include Lord Holdernesse (PRIO), whose beard is long, dwindling, and vivid (it turns more aggressively red in his confrontation with Holmes), and Tom Bellamy (LION), whose beard is flaming red.

Our brown-bearded friends are John Ferrier (STUD) whose beard is long and dashed with white, and the man who lost his hat, Henry Baker, (BLUE) who has a pointed beard of grizzled brown.

Only Valentine Walter (BRUC) seems to be light bearded, and Mortimer Tregennis' beard (DEVI) is thin. The man of the foulest antecedents, Wilson Kemp, (ENGR), had a little pointed beard, thready and ill-nourished.

Short beard men are Enoch Drebber (short and stubbly, STUD), Patrick Cairns (short and bristled, BLAC), and James E. Dodd (just plain short, BLAN). While Inspector Gregory (SILV) has a lion-like beard, Nathan Garrideb (3GAR) has a small, projecting goat's beard, and John Turner's (BOSC) beard is tangled.

Back in the 1930's and 1940's a touring baseball team called the House of David fielded nine players wearing beards. They would have loved these guys.

By the Sweat of Their Brows

(And Eyebrows)

Despite the fanciful title, the truth is that only one Canonical character really suffered from excess brow sweat. Poor old Harry Pinner should not have read the morning paper as the Mawson and Williams fiasco caused his brow to glisten with perspiration (STOC). Other brows bunched (Don Murillo, WIST), bristled (NEIL Gibson, THOR), and crumpled with anger (Jethro Rucastle, COPP). They also knitted (Holmes, ABBE), knotted (Negretto Sylvius, MAZA), and drooped (John Turner, BOSC).

Heavy, and thick, seem to have been Dr. Watson's favorite adjectives. Characters with heavy brows include Holmes (LADY), Jonathan Small (SIGN), Reuben Hayes (PRIO), and Negretto Sylvius (MAZA), whose brows also threatened. Among the thick-browed are Beppo (SIXN), Sir Henry Baskerville (thick and black, with valor and strength, HOUN), Cecil James Barker (thick, strong and black, VALL), and thick, tufted, and overhung (Patrick Cairns, BLAC). Also in the tufty brow category are Colonel Emsworth (BLAN), Culverton Smith (tufty and sandy, DYIN), and Professor Sergius Coram (overhung and tufted, GOLD). Professor Presbury (CREE) had shaggy brows, Dr. Leslie Armstrong's (MISS) are thatched, and Alec MacDonald (VALL) had great, bushy, sandy eyebrows bunched into a yellow tangle. That celebrity beauty of the day who that obnoxious blackmailer, Charles Augustus Milverton, (CHAS) had strong, dark eyebrows.

Brother Morris from Vermissa Valley (VALL) had a good brow, Inspector Baynes (WIST) has a creased brow and Mycroft Holmes' head was masterful in its brow (BRUC). Our most unlikely brow though, belongs to that of our air-gun expert, the old Shikari himself. Colonel Sebastian Moran, late of Her Majesty's Indian Army, who had the brow of a philosopher (EMPT).

You wouldn't want to fire a shot across his brow.

Hair

Although ACD liked things black and white, clearly delineated, that is, a great many of his Canonical characters have hair color somewhere in between; grizzled. Gray heads include Mrs. Peter Carey (BLAC), Professor Moriarty (FINA), and Evan Pott (VALL). Helen Stoner (SPEC) and Lord Holdhurst (NAVA) are prematurely gray, Don Murillo (WIST) has iron gray hair, and Henry Wood's (CROO) hair is shot with gray.

The grizzled (really the same as gray) are: Toller (COPP), Bannister (3STU), J.P. Trevor (GLOR), John Turner (BOSC), Charles Augustus Milverton (CHAS), Professor Presbury (CREE), and Leon Sterndale (DEVI). Robert St. Simon (NOBL) has grizzled hair around the edges and thin upon the top. Susan Cushing's (CARD) grizzling curves down her temples, Ted Baldwin (VALL) has slightly grizzled hair, Josiah Amberley (RETI) has grizzled, snaky locks, and Henry Baker's (BLUE) recently cut hair is grizzled and anointed with lime cream.

Some of the white heads are: Alexander Holder (BERY), Sergius Coram (GOLD), Mr. Frankland (HOUN), Hilton Cubit's local surgeon (DANC), and that unfortunate publisher, James Stanger (VALL).

The black heads include Neville St. Clair (TWIS), Hatty Doran (NOBL), Sophie Kratides (GREE), Jonathan Small (SIGN, curly and shot through with gray), and Enoch Drebber (crisp, curling, STUD). Annie Harrison (NAVA) has a wealth of deep black hair, Mr. Melas's (GREE) is coal black, and Adelbert Gruner (ILLU) and Boss McGinty (VALL) both have the raven variety, with the boss's being tangled. Our favorite missing person, Hosmer Angel, has black hair but was a little bald in the center. Baldies include Dr. Schlessinger (LADY), Culverton Smith (DYIN), Nathan Garrideb (3GAR), Baron Von Herling (LAST), and the brothers Sholto who are half bald with shining scalps and a bristle of red hair. And speaking of redheads, we have Tom Bellamy (florid, LION), Ezekiel Hopkins (REDH) of Lebanon, Pa., Duncan Ross (REDH) of Pope's Court, and Jabez Wilson (REDH) of Saxe-Coburn Square, the latter with a mop of blazing, fiery red. Hugh Boone (TWIS) also has bright red hair too, or is orange?

The largest category is blond and fair (meaning light), flaxen or golden. The blonds are the German manager of Gelder and Co. (SIXN), Mary Marston (SIGN), Miss Morrison (CROO), and Etta Shafter (VALL), while the golden haired characters include Baby Ferguson (SUSS), Lucy Ferrier (STUD), Mary Frazer (ABBE), Mrs. Neville St. Clair (TWIS), and Mrs. Godfrey Staunton (MISS), whose locks are tangled. Those with flaxen colored hair are: Tobias Gregson (STUD), Big Bob Ferguson (SUSS), Gilchrist (3STU), John Hector McFarlane (NORW), Jack Stapleton (HOUN), and Carry Evans (SHOS). The fair headed are Jackie Ferguson (SUSS) and Peter Carey's long suffering daughter (BLAC). Did blonds have more fun? Sorry, not here.

People with brown hair are John Ferrier (STUD), Grace Dunbar (THOR), John McMurdo (VALL), and Beryl Stapleton

(HOUN), whose hair is darker than any English brunette Watson has ever seen.

Arthur Pinner's (STOC) hair is dark but without a special color, as is Mary Holder's (BERY). Laura Lyon's hair matches her eyes, a rich hazel (a Canonical rarity, HOUN), Inspector Gregory has (lion-like hair, SILV), and harpooner Hugh Patin has lank locks (BLAC). Brigham Young (STUD) and resident patient Blessington have sandy tresses, with the latter's being thin.

Fugitives from any tonsorial establishments are: Beppo (matted, SIXN), Selden (matted, HOUN), Colonel Valentine Walter (unkempt, BRUC), and Tonga (tangled, disheveled, SIGN). Sam Merton has a short-cropped pate (MAZA) and Roaring Jack Woodley's hair is plastered down on each side of his forehead.

Obviously, the most famous hair in the Canon, somewhat luxuriant and of a rather peculiar tint of chestnut, belongs to Violet Hunter (COPP).

In her case it was hair today, gone tomorrow.

What Cheek!

Florid, flushed and ruddy is not the name of a firm of Dickensian solicitors. They do represent however, some of Dr. Watson's favorite adjectives in describing Canonical cheeks. The flushed include Peterson the commissionaire (BLUE), Alice Turner (BOSC) and the Master himself, who had a hectic flush upon either cheek in DYIN. The ruddy include James Lancaster (BLAC) and Joseph Harrison (NAVA), while Hilton Cubitt (DANC) holds down the florid look. Jephro Rucastle (COPP) had red cheeks as did Henry Baker (BLUE) who had a touch of red in both his nose and his cheeks.

We have four characters with sallow cheeks: Holmes (FIVE), Hugh Pattin (BLAC), Neil Gibson (THOR) and cheerful old Lord Cantlemere in (MAZA). A couple of white-cheeked people show up with James Ryder (BLUE), and our swindler friend Harry Pinner (STOC) whose cheeks were the dull dead white of a fish's belly. Yuccch. Fitzroy McPherson (LION) had dreadful livid cheeks and Holmes (SIGN) had a little fleck of feverish color on either cheek. The Reverend Dr. Shlessinger (LADY) had pendulous cheeks, Sidney Johnson's (BRUC) were haggard, Inspector Baynes (WIST) sported heavy creases of cheek, and traitorous Colonel Valentine Walter (BRUC) had stained cheeks.

Lady Hilda Trelawney Hope (SECO) had lovely cheeks that paled with emotion, but the winning description belongs to

Laura Lyon (HOUN). Dr. Watson went as far overboard as Jack Douglas (VALL) with this one. "Her cheeks, though considerably freckled, were flushed with the exquisite bloom of the brunette, the dainty pink which lurks at the heart of the sulphur rose."

Now that's cheek!

Jaw, Jaw, Jaw

ACD used only one pejorative among all his descriptions of Canonical jaws. Enoch Drebber, no beauty he, had a prognathous jaw (STUD). All the other jaws had indications of virile strength, such as square-jawed (Watson, CHAS; James M. Dodd, BLAN), strong-jawed (Jack Douglas, VALL), lean-jawed (Jack Stapleton, HOUN), and nut-cracker jawed (Jack Prendegast, GLOR). Dr. Leslie Armstrong (MISS) had the granite molding of the inflexible jaw, and the man with the air rifle, Colonel Sebastian Moran (EMPT), had the jaw of the sensualist.

Canonical chins ran to flesh. No less than four characters had weight problems, showing it in the chin department. Jephro Rucastle (COPP) had a great heavy chin, Mr. Ferguson (ENGR) had a double chin, Culverton Smith (DYIN) had a heavy double chin, and Thorneycroft Huxtable (PRIO) had rolling chins. Jonathan Small's chin was aggressive (SIGN), Hugh Boone had a bulldog chin (TWIS), and John Douglas' was square and projecting (VALL). Charles Augustus Milverton's assassin had a strong, little chin (CHAS), Eugenia Ronder had a delicately rounded chin (VEIL), and Anna Coram stuck out a long and obstinate chin (GOLD). One character had a long, straight chin. He was no other than Wilhelm Gottsreich Sigismond von Ormstein, Grand Duke of Cassel-Felstein, and hereditary King of Bohemia (SCAN). You may address him as the Count Von

Kramm. Wait a minute. Didn't someone write an opera about him?

Of course. La Boheme!

Ear, Ear (Earrings, Too)

Three pair of the best known Canonical ears had holes in them. Vincent Spaulding, the amateur photographer, had his ears pierced by a Gypsy when he was but a lad (REDH), Mary Cushing Browner (CARD) had finely formed ears, also pierced, and the dashing, swaggering Alec Fairbairn had pierced, sunburned, discolored ears (CARD). We can only guess whether Susan Cushing and Mary Sutherland had pierced ears but Susan did wear little gild earrings (CARD) and Mary's earrings were small, round, hanging ones (IDEN). Other different looks include lop-eared Pompey (MISS), the flattened and thickened ears of J.P. Trevor (GLOR) and the torn or jagged ear of the Reverend Dr. Shlessinger (LADY).

Ear, ear.

Skin Deep

Some Canonical characters had ghastly looking skin. Carter (VALL) had yellow parchment skin, Colonel Elias Openshaw's skin was the color of putty (FIVE), Colonel Emsworth, the Crimean V.C., had smoky skin (BLAN). The deceased Ted Baldwin's skin was lard colored (VALL) and Nathan Garrideb had the dull, dead skin of a man to whom exercise is unknown (3GAR). Jonathan Small had a good deal of skin missing from the palm of his hand (SIGN) and the nervous Mr. Blessington's skin hung about his face in loose pouches, like the cheeks of a bloodhound (RESI). John Ferrier had brown-parchment-like skin (STUD) and Jack Croker had skin burned by tropical suns (ABBE). One character's skin made for a case. He had curious, whitish patches which had bleached his skin. I refer, of course, to Lance Corporal Godfrey Emsworth of B Squadron, who suffered from a well-marked case of pseudo-leprosy or ichthyosis, a scale-like affection of the skin, unsightly, obstinate, but possibly curable and certainly non-infective (BLAN).

Enough to make a mother faint.

Let's Face It

Red, White and Pale. Although that sounds like the flag of an emerging nation those colors really represent the major descriptions of Canonical faces, although not in that order. They should read Pale, Red and White, but that doesn't sound as good.

Anyway, ACD has more facial descriptions by far than any other feature. The largest category is pale (forty-four, including pallor, and ashy), with red second (at twenty-seven), if we include crimson, ruddy, rubicund, flushed and florid. The last three sound like a firm of Dickensian solicitors - Rubicund, Flushed and Florid.

The third, mentioned twenty-six times, is white, which includes blanched. The most blanched of all was, of course, Godfrey Emsworth (BLAN), but we also have Julia Stoner (SPEC), who was blanched with terror, and Miss Burnet (WIST), who was blanched with the passion of her hatred. And some of the white faces were not just white. They were dead white (Holmes, EMPT); drawn and white (Holmes, ILLU); deadly white (Elsie Cubitt, DANC); ghastly white (Lord Holdernesse, PRIO); white as a piece of paper (Mary Cushing, CARD); white as a sheet (Dr. Richards, DEVI); white as cheese, fish-belly whiteness (Godfrey Emsworth, BLAN); white with rage (Colonel Emsworth, BLAN); and white as his necktie (Lord Mount-James, MISS). The plain white include Walters, the policeman (WIST); Tobias Gregson (STUD); Bannister (3STU); Nancy

Barclay (CROO); Violet Westbury (BRUC); John Turner (BOSC); Percy Phelps (NAVA); Ames and Mrs. Allen (VALL); Thorneycroft Huxtable (PRIO); Holmes (VALL); Barrymore (HOUN); Kitty Winter (ILLU); and James Windibank (IDEN).

Among those with red faces are: Mrs. Mordecai Smith (SIGN); Morse Hudson (SIXN); Mr. Sandeford (SIXN); Mr. Frankland (HOUN); Athelney Jones (SIGN); and Shinwell Johnson (ILLU). Then we have dusky red (Leon Sterndale, DEVI; Sir Henry Baskerville, HOUN); hideous red (Jack Woodley, SOLI); angry red (Boss McGinty, VALL); red and angry (Lestrade, NORW); fat, red (Mr. Baynes, WIST); and large, red (Reverend Dr. Shlessinger, LADY). In the ruddy department we have Hall Pycroft (STOC), Martha (LAST), and White Mason (VALL), who manages to be two colors at once, white and red. Among the crimsons are Thorneycroft Huxtable, who was crimson with shame (PRIO), and Dr. Leslie Armstrong, who was crimson with fury (MISS). The unnamed inspector from 3GAB was rubicund, and Jabez Wilson had a florid face (REDH), as did Jefferson Hope (STUD). Brigham Young's face was flushed (STUD); Von Bork flushed crimson (LAST); the Gelder & Co.'s manager (SIXN) and Sir Henry Baskerville (HOUN) had faces flushed with anger. Holmes' face in BOSC was flushed and darkened; in SCAN it became inflamed.

Here are the pale faced: John Openshaw (FIVE); James Windibank (IDEN); Godfrey Staunton's visitor (MISS); Mrs. Rucastle (COPP); Archie (REDH); Neville St. Clair and Hugh Boone, (TWIS); Percy Phelps (NAVA); Lady Brackenstall and Teresa Wright (ABBE); Ms. Carey (BLAC); Barrymore

(HOUN); Jackie Ferguson (SUSS); Ettie Shafter (VALL); and Professor Moriarty (FINA).

Beyond the pale we find Ivy Douglas (VALL), Emilia Lucca (REDC), and Mortimer Tregennis (DEVI), who are all pale and drawn. Holmes is not only pale and drawn (MAZA), but also pale and eager (THOR); pale and harassed (NORW); pale and hollow-eyed (LADY); pale and grim (NAVA); and pale and thin (FINA). Rachell Howells was pale and wan (MUSG) and Isa Whitney was pale and haggard (TWIS). Nancy Barclay (CROO), Brother Morris (VALL), Mary Holder (BERY), and Godfrey Emsworth (BLAN) are all deadly pale. More palefaces include: James Wilder (pale & agitated, PRIO); Percy Trevelyan (pale, tapered, RESI); Madame Charpentier (pale and distressed, SIGN); Joseph Stangerson (long, pale, STUD); Robert St. Simon (pale, pleasant, cultured, NOBL); Silas Brown (ashy pale, SILV); Mr. Roundhay (ashy, which means pale and wan, DEVI); Alexander Holder (ashen, BERY); Mrs. Godfrey Staunton (pale, calm, MISS); Kitty Winter (pale, intense, IDEN); and Reginald Musgrave (pale, keen, MUSG).

Pallor is unnatural paleness, and here we have John Hopley Neligan (deadly pallor, BLAC - you can't blame him); Fitzroy Simpson (extreme pallor, SILV - you can't blame him either); and Lord Holdernesse (dead pallor, PRIO. I guess you could blame him).

Before getting into certain facial expressions, let's deal with the rest of the colors. Jonathan Small (SIGN) had mahogany features. Annie Harrison (NAVA) had an olive complexion, as did Mr. Melas (GREE). Steve Dixie's face was leaden, or grey (3GAB); Holmes was grey with anger and mortification dealing with Charles Augustus Milverton (CHAS), and was bronzed by the sun in HOUN. Among the brown-faced are: J.P. Trevor (GLOR), Dolores (SUSS), John Ferrier (SIGN), and Hudson (GLOR). Richard Brunton's countenance, in death, was liver colored (MUSG). Our yellow faces include: Grimesby Roylott (SPEC); Mr. Norlett (SHOS); Selden (yellow, evil, HOUN); Culverton Smith (great yellow, DYIN); Don Juan Murillo (yellow and sapless, WIST); and John Hebron's little girl, Lucy, when she wore her mask (YELL). Sallow is a pale, sickly yellowish color, and here we find the Malay attendant (TWIS); Bob Carruthers (SOLI, dark sallow); Sam Merton (sallow, slab-sided, MAZA); and Beppo (hideous sallow, SIXN). Harry Pinner's puss was slate colored (STOC), and Hugh Boone's was black as a tinker (TWIS). We also have a host of dark faces: Emilia Lucca (REDC), Godfrey Norton (SCAN), Watson (STUD), Tiger Cormac (VALL), Mortimer Tregennis (DEVI), Brenda Tregennis (dark, clear-cut, DEVI), the Russian nobleman's son (dark, fierce, RESI), Madame Fournaye (dark, frantic, SECO), and Henry Wood (dark and fearsome, CROO). Seven swarthy-faced characters are: Reuben Hayes (PRIO), Boss McGinty (VALL), Giuseppe Gorgiano (REDC), Colonel Sebastian Moran (EMPT), Henry Wood (CROO), Abe Slaney (DANC), and Adelbert Gruner (ILLU).

We have one gaping, staring face (Holmes, LADY); one ghastly face (James Windibank, IDEN); one shame-faced (also angry faced, John Garrideb, 3GAR); three faces of granite (Holmes,

CHAS; John McMurdo, Cecil James Barker, VALL); three grave countenances (Lestrade, SIXN; Colonel Ross, SILV; John Douglas, VALL); four sharp-faced (Francis Hay Moulton, NOBL; Mike Scanlan, VALL; Lord Holdhurst, NAVA; Breckinridge, BLUE); five gaunt visages (Colonel Sebastian Moran, EMPT; Lord Bellinger, gaunt, ascetic, SECO; Holmes, gaunt, wasted, DYIN; gaunt and eager REDC; Mrs. Carey, gaunt and deep-lined, BLAC); and a baker's dozen with haggard looks: the old lodge keeper (ABBE); Percy Phelps (NAVA); Cyril Overton (MISS); Percy Trevelyan (RESI); Holmes (DEVI, DANC, and SIGN); Mrs. John Straker (SILV); Mrs. Peter Carey (BLAC); Lady Brackenstall (ABBE); John Ferrier (SIGN); Isa Whitney (TWIS); and Cecil James Barker (VALL).

Some characters had very different faces, mostly unpleasant. Here we have: acid-faced (Hudson, GLOR); aged and withered (Rose Spender, LADY); perfectly blank and rigid (the phony Russian nobleman, RESI); a prizefighter's face (Cecil James Barker, VALL); vacuous (Mary Sutherland, IDEN); brutal, heavy-faced, coarse and puffy (Roaring Jack Woodley, SOLI); coarse (Mrs. Tangey, NAVA); convulsed (Lord Holdernesse, also cadaverous, PRIO); cadaverous (Nathan Garrideb, 3GAR); horrified (Emilia Lucca, REDC); emaciated (Miss Burnet, WIST); fierce (Leon Sterndale, DEVI; Jonathan Hope STUD; Patrick Cairns, BLAC); grim, deep-lined, remorseless, hard, (J. Neil Gibson, THOR); hard (Perkins, HOUN); hatchet-faced (Lord Cantlemere, MAZA; Mr. Leverton, REDC); heavy, sullen (William Bellamy, LION); cruel (Giuseppe Gorgiano, REDC, Ted Baldwin, VALL); dour (Watson, VALL); drawn and distorted (Fitzroy McPherson, LION); drawn and thin (Lord Holdernesse, PRIO); extraordinarily malignant (Professor Presbury, CREE); seared with a thousand wrinkles (Grimesby Roylott, SPEC); pinched and fallen (Alexander Holder, BERY); most melancholy (Horace Harker, SIXN); odious (Jonas Oldacre, NORW); sad (Mortimer Tregennis, DEVI; Mrs. Marker, GOLD); sad, terribly agitated, disfigured by a horrible scar (Hugh Boone, TWIS); unhealthy (Percy Trevelyan, RESI); sour (Mrs. Toller, COPP); crinkled and puckered like a withered apple (Henry Wood, CROO); sulky (Susan Stockdale, 3GAB); sinister (Colonel Sebastian Moran, EMPT); hideous (Tonga, SIGN; Hugh Boone, TWIS); and swollen, congested (Mr. Melas, GREE; Paul Kratides, GREE).

We have several animal faces, with rat the most popular (Mr. Norlett, SHOS; Lestrade, STUD; James Ryder, BLUE; Evans Pott, VALL). We also have faces like a monkey (Jonathan Small, SIGN); a vulture (Harraway, VALL); a bulldog (Patrick Cairns, BLAC); a fox (Mortimer Tregennis, DEVI); a snarling dog (John McMurdo, VALL); and a baboon (Beppo, SIXN).

Are there any nice faces at all? Of course.

Elise (eager and beautiful, ENGR); Emilia Lucca (beautiful, REDC); Susan Cushing (placid, CARD); Irene Adler (most beautiful, a face that a man might die for, SCAN); Beryl Stapleton (finely cut, expressive, HOUN); Violet Hunter (bright, quick, freckled like a plover egg, COPP); Isadora Klein (lovely, 3GAB); Maud Bellamy (perfect, clear cut, LION); Grace Dunbar (clear cut and yet sensitive, THOR); Mary Morstan (refined and sensitive, SIGN); Hatty Doran (full, striking, NOBL); Mary Sutherland (broad, good-humored, IDEN); and Lady Francis Carfax (statuesque, LADY).

And there are pleasant looks among the men, too: Stanley Hopkins (alert, eager, ABBE); Hall Pycroft (frank, honest, STOC); Andrews (frank-faced and cheerful, VALL); John McMurdo (fresh-complexioned, VALL); Billy (fresh and smiling, MAZA); Cecil James Barker (bold, handsome, expressive, VALL); Vincent Spaulding (boyish, REDH); Cartwright (bright, keen, HOUN); Henry Baker (intelligent, BLUE); Hilton Cubitt (comely, DANC); Watson (honest, MAZA); Brother Morris (kindly, VALL); Gilchrist (pleasant, open, 3STU); Jephro Rucastle (very smiling, COPP); and Victor Hatherley (strong, masculine, ENGR).

The facial category is so large that I may have missed some, but we have enough now to call it quits.

One of the most interesting Canonical characters, half-villain, half to be admired and pitied, had the most facial descriptions. He was bearded, hairy, sunburned, and his monkey-faced features had an expression of concentrated malevolence. He was our one-legged seeker of hidden treasures, a man deeply committed to written contracts - Mr. Jonathan Small (SIGN).

They had faces then.

Mouthing Off

Petulant, hideous, cruel, vicious, drawn and grim. These are some of ACD's adjectives in describing Canonical mouths. The noble bachelor, Robert St. Simon, had something perhaps of petulance about the mouth (NOBL), and Eliza Barrymore's mouth had a stern, set expression (HOUN). Steve Dixie had a hideous mouth (3GAB), and the cruel mouths belonged to the Reverend Shlessinger (also vicious, LADY), Count Negretto Sylvius (MAZA), and the charming Baron Adelbert Gruner (ILLU), who had a murderer's mouth, a cruel hard gash in the face, compressed, inexorable and terrible. Brrrr.

Lady Hilda Trelawney Hope (SECO) had a sensitive mouth but it was tight and drawn. No wonder. John Hector McFarlane (NORW) also had a sensitive mouth but his was weak. The scarred Eugenia Ronder (VEIL) had a perfectly shaped mouth, and Hatty Doran's was exquisite (NOBL). Reuben Hayes (PRIO) had good reason to have a grim mouth, Hugo Baskerville (HOUN) had a firm-set mouth, and the lady who did in Charles Augustus Milverton (CHAS) had a straight, thin lipped mouth set in a dangerous smile.

We seem to have only one humorous mouth in the Canon and that belonged to John Douglas (VALL), but two characters are foul-mouthed. Actually one is and the other would be if he continued to malign the good name of Professor Moriarty. I refer to Jack Woodley who was (SOLI) and Dr. Watson, who would be (VALL).

Within those Canonical mouths are Canonical teeth, both white, yellow, chattering and false. The last named belonged to Mr. Dundas who used to hurl them at his wife prior to their separation (IDEN). The white teeth category includes the coal black negress with the yellow face (YELL), Sir Eustace Brackenstall (ABBE), and the mulatto cook (WIST), who had a line of white teeth like a hungry beast. The yellow, irregular variety belonged to Hudson (GLOR) and Thaddeus Sholto (SIGN); Tonga's (SIGN) were yellow and strong. Grant Munro (YELL) had an excellent set of teeth, but Harry (and Arthur) Pinner (STOC) did not. They (he) had a second tooth on the left hand side badly stuffed with gold. Our chatterer was John Hopley Neligan (BLAC) and Hugh Boone (TWIS) had a decent set of teeth but three of them were exposed in a perpetual snarl.

He was a bit long in the tooth.

Shoulder to Shoulder

The human shoulder, as Dr. Watson well knew, is composed of the clavicle, acromion, scapula, and the humerus bones. This Canonical area, when described, was almost always broad, bowed, or rounded. The elder Randall (ABBE) had broad shoulders, so did Cecil James Barker (VALL) and Cyril Overton (MISS). Big Bob Ferguson's shoulders were bowed (SUSS) as were John Turner's (BOSC). Rounded shoulder characters included Anna Coram (GOLD), Henry Baker (BLUE), Wilson Kemp (GREE), and a couple from royalty, Lord Cantlemere (MAZA) and Lord Holdernesse (PRIO). Far from royal were the shoulders of Professor Moriarty, and his were rounded from much study (FINA). Old Sherman (SIGN) had stooping shoulders, Culverton Smith (DYIN) had twisted shoulders, and Josiah Amberly's shoulders (and chest) had the framework of a giant (RETI).

The most famous Canonical shoulder had once been struck by a Jezail bullet, which shattered the bone and grazed the subclavian artery, and that shoulder, of course, belonged to John H. Watson, M.D., late of the Army Medical Department (STUD).

The Nose Knows

Although Sir Arthur Conan Doyle apparently held no prejudices when it came describing his character's noses, his favorite proboscis, statistically speaking, was hawk-like, hooked, or aquiline, all of which are similar in appearance. Among those with this physiognomy are Sherlock Holmes (hero) Ted Baldwin, Abe Slaney, Count Negretto Sylvius, Sir Eustace Brackenstall (four villains), and Dr. Leon Sterndale, Daulat Ras, and Professor Sergius Coram (three characters). Dr. Mortimer's nose is "long like a beak," but this does not necessarily mean hooked, so we shall leave him out of this category. Although eagle-like, or hawk-like, seems to lead the league, it is no runaway. In a tie for second and third is "thin," (Sherlock Holmes, Jack Prendergast, Teddy, Colonel Sebastian Moran and Grimesby Roylott; one hero, two villains, one character and one mongoose) and "long," (Jack Prendergast, Teddy, Dr. Mortimer, Count Negretto Sylvius and the Duke of Holdernesse; one villain, three characters and one mongoose). Among people whose noses are "curved," are Ted Baldwin, Count Negretto Sylvius, the Duke of Holdernesse and the murderess of Charles Augustus Milverton (one heroine, two villains, and one character). The most peculiar category of all, in which we find Reginald Musgrave, Lord Robert St. Simon, Lord Bellinger and Grimesly Roylott (one villain and three characters) is "high-nosed." This description seems to defy analysis. The only high-nosed characters I have found are in the Peanuts comic strip where both Linus and Lucy Van Pelt have noses that appear to be some distance above their eyes. Several characters, including one bully, one murderess (although not a malicious one) and one of the worst villains in the Canon, have unique noses. Anna Coram, as Holmes could tell from her golden pince-nez, had a remarkably thick nose. Steve Dixie's nose was flattened, and Enoch Drebber's blunt nose fit right in with his prognathous jaw. The poor Duke of Holdernesse. Not only was his shnozz curved and long but it was grotesquely so. To offset this, Sir Henry Baskerville had sensitive nostrils (whatever that means) and Arthur Pinner had a nose that showed the "touch of the sheeny" (some know what that means). Did Conan Doyle remember from one story to another that he already had a passel of hook-nosed villains? Who knows? The answer seems even more difficult to come by than whether or not his pregnant mother was frightened by a grey-eyed man (or woman).

Some More About Eyes

Let us delve into general appearances. Rarely does Dr. Watson describe attractive orbs, although there are a few: thoughtful eyes (Inspector Baines, WIST), clear eyes (Holmes, 3GAR; Hilton Cubitt, DANC), merry eyes (Joseph Harrison, NAVA), beautiful, haunted eyes (Lady Hilda Trelawney Hope, SECO; Mrs. Bob Ferguson, SUSS) and wonderful Spanish eyes (Isadora Klein, 3GAB).

All too often descriptions fall into pejorative categories such as: frightened   (Mrs. Bob Ferguson, SUSS; Lord Eustace, Teresa Wright, ABBE; Marlow Bates, SHOS; Mr. Roundhay, DEVI), startled (Lady Hilda Trelawney Hope, SECO), suspicious and sidelong (Mrs. Lexington, NORW), brooding (Anna Coram, GOLD), sullen (Steve Dixie, 3GAB; Reuben Hayes, PRIO), fierce (Colonel Emsworth, BLAN), wild (Colonel Valentine Walter; John Hector McFarland, NORW; Harry Pinner, STOC), resentful (J. Neil Gibson, THOR), eyes (Jonathan Small, SIGN; the Hound, HOUN), angry   (Sir Robert Norberton, SHOS); glazed, sunken (Fitzroy McPherson, LION), protruding (Mr. Melas, Paul Kratides, GREE), and great, staring, goggle (the Mulatto cook, WIST).

Manly eyes include piercing (Jack Stapleton, HOUN), bright, alert (John Garrideb, 3GAR), cunning (Reuben Hayes, SILV), quick (John Douglas, VALL), stern (James E. Dodd, BLAN), dark, hungry (Ted Baldwin, VALL), steady, shining (Sir Henry

Baskerville, HOUN), and coldly intolerant (Hugo Baskerville, HOUN).

Animal eyes include ox-like (Inspector Baines, WIST), wild-beast (Guiseppe Gorgiano, REDC) and ferret (Rev. Dr. Schlessinger's wife, LADY). J.P. Cunningham has heavy eyes (REIG), poor Carlo's eyes are mournful (SUSS), Mary Sutherland's are short-sighted, Carry Evans's are impudent (3GAB), Jabez Wilson's are fat-encircled, Reuben Hayes' are ironical, John Turner's eyes are weary, and Holmes's eyes get abstracted (ABBE). Miss Morrison (CROO) has timid eyes and Mrs. Barrymore's tell tale eyes were red.

The most fascinating description belongs to our comical friend, Mr. Jephthro Rucastle, whose eyes are small, just two shining slits. They probably got that way from all of his photography work in the attic.

Paying Lip Service

Through thick and thin, blue and purple, Dr. Watson described Canonical lips. Tonga (SIGN) had thick lips, as did the King of Bohemia (SCAN). Thaddeus Sholto (SIGN) had pendulous lips (hanging down loosely), and Holmes feigned loose-lipped senility at the Bar of Gold (TWIS). Jack Stapleton (HOUN), Baron Gruner (ILLU), and Charles Augustus Milverton (CHAS) all had thin lips. The dying John Turner (BOSC), the dead Paul Kratides (GREE) and the surviving Mr. Melas (GREE), all had blue lips, while Harry Pinner's lips turned purple (STOC). Holmes's firm lips shook (3GAR), Mary Morstan's lips trembled (SIGN), and Wilson Kemp's lips (and eyelids) twitched like a man with St. Vitus's dance (GREE). Mary Holder's lips were bloodless (BERY), Holmes's lip had a cut (SOLI), and dark crusts clung to his lips (DYIN). Holmes described Baron Gruner's lips as lecherous (ILLU), and Sir James Damery (ILLU) had mobile, smiling lips.

Other smiles were mocking (MAZA), languid (3GAB), and whimsical (CREE), and Holmes smiled all of these. Charles Augustus Milverton's murderer had a deadly smile (CHAS), the dangerous Alex Cunningham (REIG) had a bright, smiling expression, while the equally dangerous John Garrideb had a broad, set smile (3GAR).

Blackmailer Milverton (CHAS) had an insufferable, frozen, smile, which beamed insincerity. Another character with a perpetual smile, this one sinister, was sailor Hudson (GLOR).

Holmes had a sympathetic smile (SCAN), Culverton Smith's was malicious and abominable (DYIN), while Bartholomew Sholto's smile (SIGN) was horrible, ghastly and inscrutable. Ted Baldwin (VALL) had an infernal smile and the bearded cyclist, Bob Caruthers (SOLI) had a pleasant smile.

The winning smile came in answer to Dr. Watson's query (STUD), "How the deuce did he know I had just come from Afghanistan?"

His companion smiled an enigmatic smile. "That's just his little peculiarity," he said. And that is the last we ever hear from the smiling Stanton.

Chapter 4

Toasts

Toast to the Sparking Plugs

"Spark," according to the 4th meaning in my Webster's Third International Dictionary, is to engage in courting: to go together as sweethearts. There is only one set of plugs who can spark according to this definition, a set of plugs that will be forever linked to a set of dottles in Holmes's before-breakfast pipe. If you were a plug would you not spark with a dottle? I certainly would.

But, oh ye of little faith. If you don't believe that inanimate objects can spark with one another I refer you to one of our greatest American philosophers, a young man from Peru, Indiana, who wrote in 1928, "People say, in Boston, even beans do it, Let's do it. Let's fall in love. Even cuckoos in their clocks do it. Let's do it. Let's fall in love."

Here's to the sparking plugs. And dottles.

Toast to the Geese

I have been asked to toast the geese. Geese? Ben Vizoskie said geese. I said goose? Ben said geese. I would have preferred toasting a goose rather than geese as there are many rhymes to fit the case: loose, noose, deuce, excuse, and in Canada there is both moose and hoose. For geese there seems to be only Edwin Meese and Pee Wee Reese. In Covent Garden, in order to get information out of Breckinridge (a Confederate general's name) about the origin of the geese, Sherlock Holmes spots a 'Pink 'un' protruding out of the salesman's pocket, sees whiskers of "that" cut, and offers a foolish bet. And by becoming Mr. Cocksure, and figuratively, the last goose in the shop, gains the name of the breeder of that special bird lost by Mr. Henry Baker.

Mrs. Oakshott of Brixton Road only sold Breckinridge 24 geese, but the stall owner told Sherlock Holmes that he could have 500 to-morrow morning. And let's not forget Jem's bird and the one Mrs. Oakshott put aside for herself, plus the goose that Peterson bought for Holmes to return to Henry Baker.

So, if our arithmetic is correct here is a toast to the 528 geese in our tale and this includes Holmes himself.

Toast to Tea

Completely baffled by Ben Vizoskie's instructions for a toast to tea I wondered just which tea he meant. Handicapped by my gender's inability to ask for directions I plunged ahead into meaningful research. Offering toasts is certainly my cup of tea but which one? Were there any Canonical tea parties, like the one in Boston? No. Did Ben mean T like in T-shirts? I can't recall any mention of Canonical underwear. Was it a golf tee he referred to? Two mentions of that but no tea in the picture. A T-bone steak, perhaps, that's American, no? Iced T? Isn't that a rapper. A lot of Canonical villains took the rap but there were no rappers, per se.

Wasn't there a wonderful movie about tea recently? Tea biscuit? No, that was Sea Biscuit.

Could Ben mean a T-square, or the 20th letter of the alphabet, or something fitting to a T, or maybe a jazzman like Jack Teagarten. Or was he referring to T abbreviations, such as territory, township, Tuesday, tackle, teaspoon, temperature, and Teaneck, N.J.

By this time you all probably feel as though you have been sipping sleepy-time tea so I shall wrap it up. High tea or low tea I can toast, but in reality, shockingly enough more Canonical characters drank tea's ancient enemy, coffee, than any other beverage. I know this since I heard a paper on the subject offered at a 3GAB meeting.

So here is a toast to that dried and prepared leaves of a shrub, thea sinensis, from which a somewhat bitter, aromatic beverage is prepared by infusion in hot water.

Take tea and see.

Toast to Emilia Lucca

Most Canonical movie buffs are already aware of Fellini's classic depiction of Sherlock Holmes's favorite detective. I refer to the film <u>La Strada</u>. But most are unaware of another cinematic gem that highlighted our favorite heroine from Brooklyn. It featured Paul Newman and won an Academy Award for George Kennedy. Fellow Sherlockians, what we have here is <u>no</u> failure to communicate. I toast our heroine whose name has been immortalized in <u>Cool Hand Lucca</u>. Here's to Emilia Lucca.

A Toast to the Master

Here is a toast to the plumber, the accountant, the sea captain, the explorer, and the spy. I refer to Harris the accountant, Escott the plumber, Captain Basil the sea captain, Sigerson, the explorer, and the Gaelic mangler of English, Altamont, the spy. They are all the same man.

But we must also toast the ostler, the venerable Italian priest, the seaman with the workhouse cough and the weak legs, the opium eater, the old book seller, the ouvrier, the ill-dressed vagabond, the nonconformist clergyman. All of these personae from a veritable Lon Chaney of Victorian London. He was all these people but most important to us, he was the best and wisest man we ever knew.

To our favorite consulting detective, the master of disguise, and the Master, Sherlock Holmes.

Doris's Toast to Dr. Watson

I don't fly. When I absolutely have to the person in the next seat has to hold my hand when we take off or land. I don't do public speaking either. That's why Bud is here. To hold my hand.

Many of us are familiar with the famous Doctors in history. Some familiarity began when we were very young and wore Dr. Denton's. We read kids' stories about Doctor Doolittle. As young adults we thrilled to the exploits of Doc Savage. Football fans had Doc Blanchard; baseball fanaticos Doc Gooden. O.K. Corralers had Doc Halliday. If you were Afro-Centric you had Doctor Schweitzer and (nod to me) Dr. Livingstone. Movie fans had Doctor Kildare and Doctor Gillespie, James Bond aficianados had Doctor No.

But Sherlockians have the most famous doctor of all. Wounded veteran of foreign wars, brave, always dependable, willing to go the extra mile, uxorious to a fault, fleet of foot, unselfish, possessor of a pawky sense of humor, and a fixed point in a changing age. In addition, with the girls he's handy.

We have met many physicians in Sherlock Holmes' cases: Leslie Armstrong, Grimesby Roylott, Leon Sterndale, James Mortimer, and many others. But there is no doubt as to who our favorite doctor is.

Ladies and gentlemen, I give you Doctor John H. Watson.

A Toast to Dr. Watson's First Wife, a Militant Feminist

I may have called you James

And some other funny names

But you really cannot blame me.

Since you're never ever home

With Sherlock do you roam

And that really does inflame me.

And you haven't been quite frank

About no money in your bank

And the loss of half your pension.

So if I call you James

Or even throw you in the Thames

It's hardly worth the mention.

A Sussex Vampire Toast

There once was a gal from Peru

Who knew precisely what to do

She sucked out curare

And said this is hairy

And whacked little Jack black and blue

She hollered que pasa

This is no lama from Lhasa

And she then single sticked him, too

At this point my inspiration vanished (like a gambler's lucky streak)

So let us hoist our glasses to toast the nearest thing we have to Count Dracula in the Canon. To Miss Lima of 1889, Mrs. Big Bob Ferguson.

Toast to Lysander Starr

Etoile. Estrella. Stern. Stella. Astro.

Tom Cruise. Madonna.

These are all stars.

But our Starr has something that they don't have.

You've heard of the three R's? Well Lysander Starr has two R's. And that is the difference.

Viva Lysander Starr (with two R's).

A Toast to Sherlock Holmes from the Members of the Canon
The Good, The Bad, And The Indifferent

I believe you are the Devil himself.

Leon Sterndale

You fiend. You clever, clever fiend. You cunning, cunning fiend.

Colonel Sebastian Moran

You are mad. You are talking insanely.

Professor Coram

You are mad, Mr. Holmes. You are mad.

Lady Hilda Trelawney Hope

For a moment I thought you had done something clever.

Joseph Harrison

Well. I never. I thought at first you had done something clever, but I see there was nothing in it after all.

Jabez Wilson

I have been expecting you to do something original. This has been done so often and what good has ever come of it.

Charles Augustus Milverton

Excuse my amusement, Mr. Holmes. But it is really funny to see you trying to play a hand with no cards in it. I don't think anyone could do it better but it is rather pathetic, all the same.

Baron Adelbert Gruner

I have heard your name, Mr. Holmes, and I am aware of your profession one of which by no means approve.

Leslie Armstrong

You are Holmes the meddler
Holmes the busybody
Holmes the Scotland Yard jack-in-office

Grimesby Roylott

You are proud of your brains. Holmes. Are you not?
Think yourself smart, don't you?
You came across someone smarter than you.

Culverton Smith

I guess your name does not frighten me, Mr. Holmes. Why you are a common burglar.

Holy Peters

Curse you, you double traitor

Von Bork

It seems to me that all the detectives of fact and fancy would be children in your hands. That's your line of life, sir.

JP Trevor

You crossed my path on the 4th of January. On the 23rd you incommoded me. By the middle of February I was seriously inconvenienced by you. At the end of March I was absolutely hampered in my plans; and now at the close of April I find myself in such a position through your continual persecution that I am in positive danger of losing my liberty.

Professor Moriarty

The characters cited have consecrated Holmes's name far above our poor power to add or detract.

The world will little note nor long remember what we say here. But it cannot forget what he did here. And there. And everywhere.

I refer to the master, Sherlock Holmes, the best and wisest man whom we have ever known.

A Toast to Sherlock Holmes

In MISS, Sherlock Holmes asks "Could he have got back to Cambridge?" This seemingly innocuous comment led some observers to think that Holmes did not know much about the neighborhood's late trains and that this weighed against his having been at Cambridge. Later on, Holmes says "Yes, I think we must <u>run down</u> to Cambridge together." Some feel that this is another indication that Holmes was an Oxford, never a Cambridge man. The latter would say I am going <u>up to</u> Cambridge, never down. But why Oxford? Why not some other, less well known, school?

In GLOR, Holmes comments that he only made one friend in the <u>two years</u> he was at college. Again, what college? And why only two years? I believe that there is an overlooked fact showing that he returned to school, perhaps in the evening, to finish his education. Embarrassed by his night classes he never mentioned them. But it seems obvious that not only did he gain a baccalaureate; he went further by 30 credits, and he did so well that the college even named his achievement after him.

Sherlock Holmes had earned <u>the very first Master's Degree</u>.

A Toast to Mycroft Holmes

It seems obvious that the Holmes family was embarrassed about certain things. Sherlock never mentioned what school he attended, the reason being, as I had noted in a previous toast, that he attended night classes. Mycroft, too, had a past he wanted hid. As a lad, he ran into trouble with the law and was told to either join her majesties forces or go to gaol. So he enlisted in the Royal Navy and actually served on HMS Pinafore.

If you recall Watson's description of him, he was much larger and stouter than Sherlock. His body was absolutely corpulent, but his face, though massive, had preserved something of the sharpness of expression which was so remarkable in that of his brother. His eyes, which were of a peculiarly light, watery grey, seemed to always retain that far-away introspective look which I had only observed in Sherlock's when he was exerting his full powers. "I am so glad to meet you, sir," said he, in GREE, putting out a broad, fat hand like the flipper of a seal.

Now that you know his background let us toast Mycroft Holmes, the Canon's one and only Navy Seal.

Chapter 5

Whatnots

The Dreaded Homework Assignment for

Mrs Hudson's Cliftdwellers

Hail the Cliffdwellers

where every one is clebber

Very truly yours,

The Mormon Enoch Drebber

A small birthday present

From an even smaller Tonga

Who offers you free

Three lessons from Madame LaZonga.

To the Cliffdwellers

Let there never be bad blood between us

Sincerely, The Sussex Vampire

Yellow Pages Directory London 1895

Accidents Arranged

Baron Adelbert Gruner, Vernon Lodge, near Kingston

Acrobatics

Jack Croker, Sydenham

Jonathan Small, c/o Jacobson's Yard, River Thames

Tonga, same address

Agents (Double)

Altamount, Fratton

Agents (German)

Von Bork, Harwich

Agricultural Machinery

Howard Garrideb, Grosvenor Buildings, Aston

Amputations (Ears)

Jim Browner, c/o S.S. May Day, Albert Dock

Amputations (Thumbs)

Colonel Lysander Stark, Eyford, Berkshire

Bankers

Alexander Holder, Fairbank, Streatham

Bank Robbers

Biddle, Hayward, Moffat, Sutton, c/o Blessington, 403 Brook Street

Bell rope Installations

Dr. Grimesby Roylott, Stoke Moran, Surrey

Bigamists

Hatty Doran Moulton St. Simon, Lancaster Gate

Blackmailers

Eduardo Lucas, Godolphin Street, Westminster

Charles Augustus Milverton, Appledore Towers, Hampstead

Bootnappers

Jack Stapleton, Merripit House, Dartmoor, Devon

Card Cheats

Colonel Sebastian Moran, Conduit Streeet

Colonel Upwood, Nonpareil Club

Catchers of Card Cheats

Honorable Ronald Adair, 327 Park Lane

Cockroach Extermination

Edward Rucastle, Copper Beeches, Hampshire

Cremations and Crypt Burials:

Sir Robert Norberton, Shoscombe Old Place, Shoscombe Park

Keys Made

Lady Hilda Trelawney Hope, Whitehall Terrace

Poker bending (forward)

Dr. Grimesby Roylott, Stoke Moran, Surrey

Poker Bending (backward)

Sherlock. Holmes, 221 B Baker Street

Treasure Chest Disposal

Jonathan Small, c/o Jacobson's Yard, River Thames

Hiding Places

Anna Coram, Yoxley Old Place, Kent

John Douglas, Birlstone Manor, Sussex

Jonas Oldacre, Deep Dene House, Lower Norwood

Murderers

Cyanea Capillata, Bathing Pool, Fulworth

Tonga's Law Suit

My name is Godfrey Norton, from the BCLU, the British Civil Liberties Union, and I represent the estate of Tonga, the deceased Andaman Islander whose civil rights were trampled upon by the official police and the amateur detective Sherlock Holmes and his assistant Dr. John H. Watson.

My client was taking a peaceful, leisurely boat ride down the River Thames in the Aurora, when he was suddenly and unprovokedly attacked by Scotland Yard detective Athelney Jones and the aforementioned Holmes and Watson, who had pursued my client in a police boat. If you, members of the jury, were suddenly and unprovokedly attacked by three men with their pistols at the ready, aiming at you, what would you have done? Why, protect yourself by any means possible. And my client, having only his trusty blowgun nearby, the blowgun that he only used to hunt monkeys and small, flightless birds in his home in the Indian Ocean, stood little chance against the firepower of the fascist thugs who attacked him. And he couldn't swim, either.

I am asking damages of 1,000 pounds for the family of the late, lamented Tonga, for his wife, Songa Tonga, and his little boy, Tonga, Jr., who happens to be even littler than Tonga, who will need large supplies of growth hormones throughout his stunted life.

I rest my case.

Clerihews

Count Sylvius (comma) Negretto

He wrote himself a libretto

Where he truly did own

The great Mazarin Stone

Poor Julia Stoner

She really pulled a boner

By a major she was smitten

By an adder she was bitten

The Bar of Gold

So I'm told

Has drugs for all

Just give'em a call

Lysander Starr

Traveled wide and far

He'd been in Eureka

But never Topeka

While the commissaire

Pulled out his hair

Bob's your uncle

It's the blue carbuncle

Thanksgiving Thanks

Mary Sutherland, for finally finding Mr. Right.

Lysander Starr, for being reelected Mayor of Topeka.

Robert St. Simon, for advice from Donald Trump on how to live within his income.

Tonga, for Louisa Mae Alcott's book, <u>Little Women.</u>

Altamont, for 10 free lessons on how to speak the King's English.

Apologies to Joe Fink

Here are some potential facts about Sherlock Holmes and his connections with women.

Don't believe all those stories about Holmes's misogyny or the tales of his not trusting women, even the best of them. Can anyone deny the connection between Holmes and the following people of the feminine persuasion?

Gloria Scott

Alicia

Sophy Anderson

Agatha

Matilda Briggs

The Old Russian Woman

Isadora Persano

Minnie Warrender

Joyce Cummings

Mrs. Turner, who according to Jack Tracey "her role in the Baker Street household is very uncertain."

What was the role of cross dressing and salacious language in the Canon? In TWIS, Holmes plucks at Watson's skirt; in REDH, Inspector Jones clutches Archie's skirts. In MAZA, Holmes admits to playing the role of an elderly woman to whom Count Negretto Sylvius handed a parasol. Irene Adler, dressed as a boy, says good night to Holmes in SCAN and in many cases there are actual ejaculations (GOLD, SPEC, REDH) from both Holmes and Watson.

What about Baron Beverly? What went on in Mincing Lane? What was Professor Moriarty doing with that young girl with a lamb? What on earth was going on in those Victorian days in Holmes's England?

The Ritz's Doorman

The Ritz's big John the doorman

Decided to take on George Foreman

The fight was one punch

And John he did crunch

Foreman: If he's a boxer I'm a Mormon.

Stangerson, Drebber and all,

Broke fast with great Mormon gall

They kidnapped a bride

Pushed Hope aside

And had a polygamous ball.

A Study beginning at Barts

Won all our Sherlockian hearts

Through Scarlet and Four

And a thrilling denouement with darts.

There once was a bullet Jezail

That took the funniest trail

It went through a shoulder

And then being bolder

Wound up in a leg near the tail.

What Ever Happened To...

Holy Peters (LADY) escaped the police and headed to Ozone Park, in Queens. His daughter Bernadette Peters, spent <u>Sundays in the Park</u> with George.

Jack Crocker (ABBE), instead of being faithful to Mary Brackenstall, nee Frazer, fell in love once more on his next ocean voyage. This time he married a woman named Betty. It was said that Betty Crocker could bake one helluva of a cake.

Dr. John Watson finally had children with his seventh wife. His granddaughter, Emma Watson, played Hermione Granger in the Harry Potter movies.

Abdullah Khan (SIGN) died in prison, but his brother's son, Sammy Kahn, not only wrote lyrics for Frank Sinatra, but also gave away the bride at his Uncle Ali Khan's wedding to Rita Hayworth.

Wilson Kemp (GREE), a man of the foulest antecedents, did not die in Buda, or even Pesth. He settled in Los Angeles with his brother, Ulysses Nathan, known as U.N. Kemp, or Un Kemp. Un's son, Jack Kemp, played quarterback for the Los Angeles Chargers.

John Sanger (VEIL), whose circus rivaled Ronder's, had a recalcitrant sister, Margaret Sanger, who was arrested in Brownsville, Brooklyn, for distributing birth control material.

Irene Adler and Godfrey Norton (SCAN) had a child who became the world's best-known underground sanitation engineer, the famous sewer worker, Ed Norton, of the Honeymooners.

Fritz Von Waldbaum (NAVA), the criminal specialist of Dantzig, opened up Von branch of his famous supermarket, Von Waldbaums Supermarket on Long Island.

Old Abrahams (LADY), tired of being in mortal terror of his life, moved to Vermissa Valley, in Pennsylvania. For a while he worked for Herman Strauss, an enemy of the Scowrers, who forced him out of business. Soon afterward, they opened a department store: Abrahams and Strauss.

Theresa Wright (ABBE) quit Mary Brackenstall's service, came to America, and was a successful Congresswoman. When asked to run for higher office she said, "I'd rather be Wright than president."

Sir Jasper Meek (DYIN), whom Watson wanted to treat his friend, the dying detective, retired soon afterwards when he came into an extraordinary inheritance. Learning that God was dead he was shocked to find his name in God's last will and testament, and as predicted, Meek inherited the earth.

Books for Canonical Characters

Altamount - Funk and Wagnall's <u>Guide to Correct English</u>

Sherlockian Colours

Captain James Calhoun of the <u>Lone Star</u> - <u>The Perfect Storm</u>

James Phillimore, who stepped back into his own house to get his umbrella and was never more seen in this world - <u>Gone With The Wind</u>.

Communists are Red

Spinach is green

Mycroft is fat

Sherlock is lean

Silas is Brown

Philip is Green

A Study in Scarlet was once

A Tangled Skein

An embarrassed face is red

A seasick one is green

Mary Morstan is good

Baron Gruner is mean

Traffic lights are red

Then they turn green

Holy Peters thinks

He is really Bishop Sheen

Quote, Unquote.

A Game Of Who Said What

"Would to God that I had given him notice on the very day that he came."

Madame Charpentier STUD

"Well, well, you must not do anything rash, or that you might repent. Let me hear all about it. Give me the facts."

Major Sholto SIGN

"Thank God. You'll do. Come! Come!"

Godfrey Norton SCAN

"We live very quietly, sir, the three of us; and we keep a roof over our heads and pay our debts, if we do nothing more."

Jabez Wilson REDH

"She was angry, and said that I was never to speak of the matter again."

Mary Sutherland IDEN

"Yes, the lodge-keeper brought it up. You said that you wished to see me here to avoid scandal."

John Turner BOSC

"Death."

Elias Openshaw FIVE

"It was very sweet of you to come. Now, you must have some wine and water, and sit here comfortably and tell us all about it."

Mrs. Watson   TWIS

"You'll never persuade me to believe that."

Sherlock Holmes BLUE

"I could not sleep that night. A vague feeling of impending misfortune impressed me."

Helen Stoner   SPEC

"Oh, my night could not be called monotonous."

Victor Hatherley   ENGR

"I really have made no inquiries on he subject."

Sir Robert St. Simon NOBL

"No doubt you will think me mad?"

Alexander Holder   BERY

"Tut, tut! This is all quite beside the question."

Jephro Rucastle COPP

"And yet, even now I fail to understand what the theory of the police can be."

Dr. Watson   SILV

"The fact is that I am a little upset, and you must put it all down to that."

Grant Munro   YELL

"This outburst rather astonished me, as you can think."

Hall Pycroft   STOC

"I've always been on my guard since then, though I have no idea how you know it."

Trevor, Sr.   GLOR

"I had myself extinguished the lamp and closed the door before coming to bed. Naturally my first thought was of burglars."

Reginald Musgrave   MUSG

"None as yet. But the affair is a petty one, one of our little country crimes, which must seem too small for your attention, Mr. Holmes, after this great international affair."

Colonel Hayter   REIG

"One or two of them are so trivial that really I am almost ashamed to mention them. But the matter is so inexplicable, and the recent turn which it has taken is so elaborate, that I shall lay it all before you, and you shall judge what is essential and what is not."

Dr. Percy Trevelyan   RESI

"To anyone who wishes to study mankind this is the spot. Look at the magnificent types!"

Mycroft Holmes   GREE

"I won't waste your time…I'll plunge into the matter without further preamble. I was a happy and successful man, Mr. Holmes, and on the eve of being married, when a sudden and dreadful misfortune wrecked all my prospects in life."

Percy Phelps   NAVA

"Well, I trust she is no worse?"

Dr. Watson   FINA

"If I am in the hands of the law, let things be done in a legal way."

Colonel Sebastian Moran   EMPT

"You musn't blame me. I am nearly mad."

John Hector McFarlane   NORW

"A promise is a promise, Mr. Holmes."

Hilton Cubitt   DANC

"I promised my friend that I would say nothing of the matter, and a promise is a promise."

Miss Morrison CROO

"I would sooner have a savage wild animal loose about the place."

Violet Smith SOLI

"Exactly. We had tried to keep it out of the papers, but there was some rumor in the <u>Globe</u> last night. I thought it might have reached your ears."

Thorneycroft Huxtable   PRIO

"Failure, sir, absolute failure."

Stanley Hopkins   BLAC

"Dear me, dear me, how unfortunate. I cannot help thinking that ladies are ill advised in not making an effort. Look at this!"

Charles Augustus Milverton   CHAS

"However, I've heard your name, Mr. Sherlock Holmes, and if you'll only explain this queer business, I shall be paid for my trouble in telling you the story."

Horace Harker   SIXN

"I am a light sleeper and so is my wife."

Trelawney Hope SECO

"The man is rather deaf, and in any case we must take our chance of that."

Sir Henry Baskerville   HOUN

"I don't know, Mr. Holmes. There may have been only one. I have not noticed them for months."

Ames, the butler   VALL

"Finally when I got your reply to my wire I came out to you, since I gather that you are a person who gives advice in difficult cases."

Scott Eccles   WIST

"I had heard that you handled strange cases, and that was why I sent to you."

Nathan Garrideb   3GAR

"It must tend to some end, or else our universe is ruled by chance, which is unthinkable.

Sherlock Holmes   CARD

"This much we can say: that it is no ordinary love escapade."

Sherlock Holmes   REDC

"Your discretion is as well known as your powers, and you are the one man in the world who can help me. I beg you, Mr. Holmes, to do what you can."

Hilton Soames 3STU

"At the same time, the gate of the garden is a hundred yards from the main London to Chatham road. It opens with a latch, and there is nothing to prevent anyone from walking in."

Stanley Hopkins   GOLD

"Yes, sir. I was standing by the door, and he with his back turned to that table. When he had written it, he said, 'All right, porter, I will take this myself.'"

The day porter MISS

"I'll chance it. I believe you are a man of your word and a white man, and I'll tell you the whole story."

Jack Crocker   ABBE

"He had saved a few hundreds, and we were to marry in the New Year."

Violet Westbury BRUC

"What is the meaning of this intrusion. Didn't I send you word that I would see you tomorrow morning?"

Culverton Smith DYIN

"Un sauvage – un veritable sauvage."

Jules Vibart   LADY

"It is the most unheard of business."

Mr. Roundhay   DEVI

"No, no, don't call it a pose. A pose is an artificial thing. This is quite natural. I am a born sportsman. I enjoy it."

Von Bork   LAST

"Everything has been done to cure her of her madness, but in vain."

Sir James Damery   ILLU

"Yes indeed. But the letter was written in the afternoon, and a good deal has happened since then."

James M. Dodd   BLAN

"There are folk who watch us from over yonder. I can see a fellow now at the window. Have a look for yourself."

Billy the page   MAZA

"I have never known anyone so vitally alive. He lived intensely – every fiber of him."

Sherlock Holmes   3GAB

"No, he cannot understand. But he should trust."

Mrs. Bob Ferguson   SUSS

"Maybe I have a clue and don't know it."

J. Neil Gibson THOR

"I really can hardly justify myself if I speak before any third person."

Jack Bennett CREE

"At your old tricks again."

Harold Stackhurst LION

"I fear I lied to him. Perhaps it would have been wiser had I told the truth."

Eugenia Ronder VEIL

"He let out a yell, and away he went as hard as he could lick it in the darkness."

John Mason SHOS

"If this is a joke, sir, it is a very questionable one."

Vicar J.C. Elman RETI

Abbreviations for the Canon Titles

Abbreviations	**Title**
3 GAB	(A) the Three Gables
3 GAR	(A) the Three Garridebs
3 STU	(A) the Three Students
ABBE	(A) the Abbey Grange
BERY	(A) the Beryl Coronet
BLAC	(A) Black Peter
BLAN	(A) the Blanched Soldier
BLUE	(A) the Blue Carbuncle
BOSC	The Boscombe Valley Mystery
BRUC	(A) the Bruce-Partington Plans
CARD	(A) the Cardboard Box
CHAS	(A) Charles Augustus
COPP	(A) the Copper Beeches
CREE	(A) the Creeping Man

CROO	The Crooked Man
DANC	(A) the Dancing Men
DEVI	(A) the Devil's Foot
DYIN	(A) the Dying Detective
EMPT	(A) the Empty House
ENGR	(A) the Engineer's Thumb
FINA	The Final Problem
FIVE	The Five Orange Pips
GLOR	The Gloria Scott
GOLD	(A) the Golden Pince-Nez
GREE	The Greek Interpreter
HOUN	The Hound of the Baskervilles
IDEN	A Case of Identity
ILLU	(A) the Illustrious Client
LADY	The Disappearance of Lady Frances Carfax
LAST	His Last Bow
LION	(A) the Lion's Mane

MAZA	(A) The Mazarin Stone
MISS	(A) the Missing Three-Quarter
MUSG	The Musgrave Ritual
NAVA	The Naval Treaty
NOBL	(A) the Noble Bachelor
NORW	(A) the Norwood Builder
PRIO	(A) the Priory School
REDC	(A) the Red Circle
REDH	The Red-headed League
REIG	The Reigate Squires (or The Reigate Puzzle)
RESI	The Resident Patient
RETI	(A) The Retired Colourman
SCAN	A Scandal in Bohemia
SECO	(A) the Second Stain
SHOS	(A) Shoscombe Old Place
SIGN	The Sign of Four
SILV	Silver Blaze

SIXN	(A) the Six Napoleons
SOLI	(A) The Solitary Cyclist
SPEC	(A) the Speckled Band
STOC	The Stockbroker's Clerk
STUD	A Study in Scarlet
SUSS	(A) the Sussex Vampire
THOR	The Thor Bridge
TWIS	The Man With the Twisted Lip
VALL	The Valley of Fear
VEIL	(A) the Veiled Lodger
WIST	(A) Wisteria Lodge
YELL	The Yellow Face

Also from MX Publishing

MX Publishing is the world's largest specialist Sherlock Holmes publisher, with over a hundred titles and fifty authors creating the latest in Sherlock Holmes fiction and non-fiction.

From traditional short stories and novels to travel guides and quiz books, MX Publishing caters for all Holmes fans.

The collection includes leading titles such as Benedict Cumberbatch In Transition and The Norwood Author which won the 2011 Howlett Award (Sherlock Holmes Book of the Year).

MX Publishing also has one of the largest communities of Holmes fans on Facebook with regular contributions from dozens of authors.

www.mxpublishing.com

Also from MX Publishing

Our bestselling short story collections 'Lost Stories of Sherlock Holmes', 'The Outstanding Mysteries of Sherlock Holmes', 'Untold Adventures of Sherlock Holmes' (and the sequel 'Studies in Legacy') and 'Sherlock Holmes in Pursuit'.

Also from MX Publishing

Sherlock Holmes and The Adventure of The Grinning Cat

"Joseph Svec, III is brilliant in entwining two endearing and enduring classics of literature, blending the factual with the fantastical; the playful with the pensive; and the mischievous with the mysterious. We shall, all of us young and old, benefit with a cup of tea, a tranquil afternoon, and a copy of Sherlock Holmes, The Adventure of the Grinning Cat."

Linda Hein, Hein & Co Used Books, and founding officer of the Amador County Holmes Hounds Sherlockian Society